The Brubaker family is back.
This time it's Big Daddy's three hunky nephews
who are in need of some good women.
And nothing is going to stop this proud patriarch
from finding the right little ladies
for his bronco bustin' boys.

THE BRUBAKER
BRIDES

THE MILLIONAIRE'S WAITRESS WIFE
(SR#1482 November 2000)

"Some little filly's got me posing as her
working-class groom. She's gonna split a gut
when she discovers her 'husband' is filthy rich."
—Dakota Brubaker

MONTANA'S FEISTY COWGIRL
(SR#1488 December 2000)

"This persistent petunia is posing as a boy—
and she thinks I don't know the truth.
Yee-haw, this is gonna be fun!"
—Montana Brubaker

TEX'S EXASPERATING HEIRESS
(SR#1494 January 2001)

"She's the one carting around a million-dollar pig
and she says *I'm* difficult to get along with?"
—Tex Brubaker

Dear Reader,

This holiday season, as our anniversary year draws to a close, we have much to celebrate. The talented authors who have published—and continue to publish—unforgettable love stories. You, the readers, who have made our twenty-year milestone possible. And this month's very special offerings.

First stop: BACHELOR GULCH, Sandra Steffen's popular ongoing miniseries. They'd shared an amazing night together; now a beguiling stranger was back in his life carrying *Sky's Pride and Joy*. She'd dreamed *Hunter's Vow* would be the marrying kind…until he learned about their child he'd never known existed—don't miss this keeper by Susan Meier! Carolyn Zane's BRUBAKER BRIDES are back! *Montana's Feisty Cowgirl* thought she could pass as just another *male* ranch hand, but Montana wouldn't rest till he knew her secrets…and made this 100% woman completely his!

Donna Clayton's SINGLE DOCTOR DADS return…STAT. *Rachel and the M.D.* were office assistant and employer…so why was she imagining herself this widower's bride and his triplets' mother? Diana Whitney brings her adorable STORK EXPRESS series from Special Edition into Romance with the delightful story of what happens when *Mixing Business…with Baby*. And debut author Belinda Barnes tells the charming tale of a jilted groom who finds himself all dressed up…to deliver a pregnant beauty's baby—don't miss *His Special Delivery!*

Thank you for celebrating our 20th anniversary. In 2001 we'll have even more excitement—the return of ROYALLY WED and Marie Ferrarella's 100th book, to name a couple!

Happy reading!

Mary-Theresa Hussey

Mary-Theresa Hussey
Senior Editor

Please address questions and book requests to:
Silhouette Reader Service
U.S.: 3010 Walden Ave., P.O. Box 1325, Buffalo, NY 14269
Canadian: P.O. Box 609, Fort Erie, Ont. L2A 5X3

Montana's Feisty Cowgirl

CAROLYN ZANE

SILHOUETTE *Romance*®

Published by Silhouette Books

America's Publisher of Contemporary Romance

For my sister in Christ
(and laughter), Liz Curtis-Higgs.

God hath made me to laugh,
so that all that hear will laugh with me.
—*Genesis* 21:6

 SILHOUETTE BOOKS

ISBN 0-373-19488-9

MONTANA'S FEISTY COWGIRL

Copyright © 2000 by Carolyn Suzanne Pizzuti

Visit Silhouette at www.eHarlequin.com

Printed in U.S.A.

Books by Carolyn Zane

*Sister Switch
†The Brubaker Brides

CAROLYN ZANE

lives with her husband, Matt, their preschool daughter, Madeline, and their latest addition, baby daughter Olivia, in the rolling countryside near Portland, Oregon's Willamette River. Like Chevy Chase's character in the movie *Funny Farm*, Carolyn finally decided to trade in a decade of city dwelling and producing local television commercials for the quaint country life of a novelist. And even though they have bitten off decidedly more than they can chew in the remodeling of their hundred-year-plus-old farmhouse, life is somewhat saner for her than for poor Chevy. The neighbors are friendly, the mail carrier actually stops at the box and the dog, Bob Barker, sticks close to home.

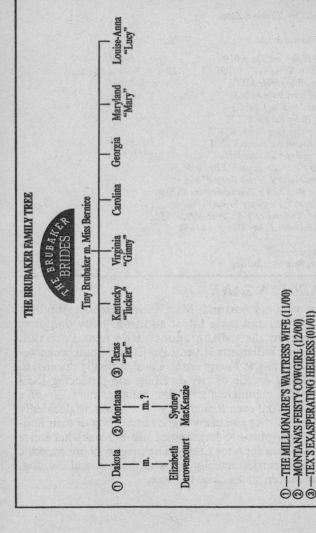

THE BRUBAKER FAMILY TREE

THE BRUBAKER BRIDES

Tiny Brubaker m. Miss Bernice

① Dakota ② Montana ③ Texas "Tex" Kentucky "Tucker" Virginia "Ginny" Carolina Georgia Maryland "Mary" Louise-Anna "Lucy"

m. — m. ?

Elizabeth Derovencourt Sydney MacKenzie

①—THE MILLIONAIRE'S WAITRESS WIFE (11/00)
②—MONTANA'S FEISTY COWGIRL (12/00)
③—TEX'S EXASPERATING HEIRESS (01/01)

Chapter One

Sydney MacKenzie gripped the edge of her skirt and, shifting her hips to and fro on the couch, tugged the hem more firmly down around her knees. Averting her eyes, she feigned rabid fascination with the multicolored pattern in the carpet and tried to appear as if she didn't notice the fact that all eyes in the waiting room to the Circle BO ranch offices were roving the curves of her legs.

When her head began to swim from staring at the carpet, she rechecked—for the dozenth time in less than an hour—the contents of the manila folder that lay in her lap. Everything was still in order. Her résumé was impressive and professional, as were her letters of recommendation, references and copies of awards and degrees.

If paper was anything to go by she had a good chance at the job. If the competition was any indication—she noted the staring, slobbering faction in her peripheral vision—she already had the job and could start today. Certainly, she had nothing to fear from these sorry excuses for job applicants.

The designer interior of the opulent Brubaker main ranch office was a stark study in contrast to the men who sat fidgeting in the chairs nearby. The stench of alcohol on the breath of the undoubted criminal, seated to her left, rivaled his body odor. To her right, a bowlegged, stoop-shouldered man who could easily have been her grandfather struggled to adjust the high-pitched squeal of his hearing aid. Across the room, three leering men mentally undressed her and a fourth, his jaw slack, his eyes rolled back in his head, snored in some sort of anti-rhythm to the cool, piped-in jazz music.

Yes, she had a good shot at this job.

Though she knew it by heart, Sydney moved her gaze to the advertisement she'd torn from the Sunday classifieds.

Wanted: Ranch Hand/Foreman Assist. Full-time, perm. Exper.w/ working cattle ranch, & some lrg animal med. Ed in Ranch Mgmt a real plus. No stdnts for sumr job, pls. Must be 18. Exclnt wage, bnfts & hsing. Apply: Circle BO Ranch Offices, Hidden Valley, TX.

This certainly described her to a tee. Again she glanced around and wondered about the qualifications of the other applicants in the room. Woman or not, surely she was the best candidate for the job. She had to be.

With a desperation she'd never known before, Sydney once again read the part about excellent wages, benefits and housing. Excellent wages were about the only way she'd ever pay off the litany of debt she owed. She had to get this job. It was do or die.

Sydney took a deep breath and gave herself a mental pep talk. She'd done everything in her power to make a good impression. Her suit, though aging and somewhat out of style, was clean and well pressed. She'd applied a subtle hint of makeup and spent some precious money to have her hair salon-styled and her nails done. She looked good. Professional. As if she'd given this interview some thought.

And she had.

She'd thought of nothing else since Sunday. Well-paying ranch hand jobs were very hard to come by in these parts. The fact that there was even an ad in the paper was nothing short of a miracle.

Startled back to the moment by the sound of the door to the inner office opening, Sydney tensed as a man's voice called her name.

"MacKenzie?"

She could feel all eyes on her as she stood, gathered her materials and strode purposefully across the room.

"That's me."

She held out her hand and it was enveloped in a strong grip. Vaguely she was aware that the man who greeted her was devastatingly handsome, with his dark shock of hair falling rakishly over his forehead and eyes so deep blue a girl could get the bends if she stared too long. Just her luck. It would have been far easier if he'd been ugly. She disentangled her hand from his and took a deep breath to soothe her jangled nerves.

"I'm Montana Brubaker. Nice to meet you—" there was a note of surprise in his voice as he checked his clipboard then allowed his gaze to travel back to her "—Ms. MacKenzie." Just behind his friendly dimples, there was the tiniest hint of irritation and impatience in his expression.

Sydney had seen this look before. Obviously he wasn't expecting a woman. Didn't think she could do the job. She rotated her shoulders. Minor obstacle. Soon she would have him eating out of the palm of her hand. She flashed him a thousand-watt smile. "Thank you. Please. Call me Sydney."

"Cindy. Okay. Great. Come on in."

"I...uh...it's Syd—" she brushed past him into the cool, ultrachic interior of his office "—ney."

"Cindy, this is my uncle, Big Daddy Brubaker."

"Well, howdy theyah," a deep voice boomed as the swivel chair behind the huge mahogany desk spun around, revealing a diminutive man in a ten-gallon hat that appeared to have swallowed his head. "Pleased to meet up with ya...Cindy." Big Daddy leapt out of his chair to enthusiastically attack Sydney's hand.

"Sydney." She smiled, hoping to smooth the name correction.

"Cindy."

"*Syd*ney."

"Right. First names are preferable to me, too. So, Cindy. Good. Have a seat."

Okay. No use belaboring the point. The pronunciation of her name was not at issue here. Job qualifications were. She moved to the front of the desk and took one of a pair of leather club chairs. Montana took the other. She balanced her folder on her knees and waited a moment for everyone to get settled.

The office walls were adorned with various rodeo pictures of good-looking, strapping cowboys frozen in time on the backs of furiously bucking bulls and horses. The Brubaker wall of fame, she surmised, impressed. The glass cases behind the desk held a vast array of trophies and ribbons. Other framed awards, certificates and college degrees cluttered the floor-to-ceiling bookshelves on the opposite wall.

Sydney tried to appear nonchalant, but it was tough.

Working for the illustrious Brubaker family would be a dream come true.

"Okay, Cindy. Why are you here, honey?" Big Daddy's puzzled frown took her aback.

Why was she here? What an odd question. "I…uh…"

"Big Daddy, I think Cindy is applying for the ranch hand job. Is that right, Cindy?" Montana's warm smile gave her confidence.

"Yes." She sat up a little straighter.

"Oh." Big Daddy scratched his jaw. "It was the clothes that threw me, I guess."

Sydney felt the tips of her ears grow hot. "I'd be dressed this way if I were interviewing for a janitorial position or a secretarial position. I believe in putting my best foot forward in any job interview."

"And you have."

There was approval in Montana's voice, and she found herself relaxing. "Anyway, I saw your ad in the paper, and I feel that I have the experience and qualifications for the job." She held out her folder to Big Daddy. "If you'll just take a moment, I think you'll see—"

"Right. Sure." The older man took the folder and, setting it on the ink blotter before him, crossed his hands over the top. "Paper is so impersonal. Go ahead, honey. Tell us in your own words why you feel you are qualified for the job."

Caught off guard by his dismissal of her carefully prepared presentation, Sydney groped for a jumping-off point.

"Uh…okay. Well, let's see now…" Holding up a hand, she began ticking her accomplishments off on her fingers. "For starters, I have lived on a working cattle ranch all my life. My family has owned the MacKenzie Cattle Company, up near College Station, for three generations. I attended A&M on a rodeo scholarship. I had a double major in range

science and animal husbandry, with a strong minor in business management.''

Brows cocked, Montana and Big Daddy exchanged
glances that told her she was beginning to catch their attention.

''My résumé goes over my extracurricular activities in
more detail, but some of the highlights include membership
in the Horsemen's Association, Ag Council, Management
Society, Pre-Vet Society, Saddle and Sirloin, Soil Conser-
vation Society, Who's Who, editor of the Aggieland year-
book, president of the Rodeo Club and—'' she paused for
air ''—I served on MSC Town Hall.''

Eyes wide, the men once again glanced at each other.

''After I earned my bachelor's, I applied for the pre-vet
program and was accepted into the department of large animal medicine and surgery, but for financial reasons I had
to take a...sabbatical of sorts. My father was a large animal
veterinarian, as well as a rancher, and when I still lived at
home, I helped him care for our purebred stock. My entire
life revolves around working on a ranch.''

Clearly impressed, Montana stroked his lower lip and
studied her when he wasn't darting furtive glances at his
uncle. Taking this as a good sign, Sydney forged ahead
with renewed enthusiasm.

''Even my hobbies reflect my interest in ranching, as you
will see on my—'' she pointed to the file, still locked under
Big Daddy hands ''—résumé. I've listed my awards in
breakaway roping, calf roping, team roping and barrel and
pole racing. Sharpshooting is another avocation of mine, as
you will note by the newspaper article I've enclosed.''

''Well now—'' Big Daddy cleared his throat ''—that's
pretty durned impressive. Forgive me, lamb chop, for wondering why don't you work for your mama and daddy's
spread anymore?''

Sydney hesitated, wondering how to couch the truth so that it wouldn't get her into trouble somewhere down the road. She wanted to keep her failing ranch out of the discussion. "My parents no longer own the ranch and due to financial difficulties, the new owner can't afford any help."

Montana propped his elbows on his knees and, hands dangling between his legs, leaned toward her. "I have to wonder why someone with your qualifications isn't running a ranch somewhere else, then. Why do you want a foreman's assistant ranch hand job?"

Because it's all that's available, she wanted to scream. *Because I'm on the verge of losing my spread and I'm desperate for the money. Because all the really good ranch management jobs are currently taken by a bunch of less qualified men.*

But she couldn't do that. Instead, she donned a confident smile and told a partial truth. "Because I see this position as an opportunity to hone my skills. Someday, I hope to run my own ranch." *Again.* She smiled so hard the cords in her neck began to throb and her back teeth started to ache.

The ensuing silence was deafening. Sydney racked her brain for something else that would convince them that she was the only candidate for the job.

Montana dragged a hand over his shadowed jaw. Big Daddy pursed his lips and thumped a pencil's eraser tip against the desk blotter in a noisy staccato. The wall clock tick-tocked the seconds away.

Sydney clenched and unclenched her fingers. This suspense was murder. The temptation to oversell herself was strong. But she knew she'd done a good job. Anything more would be gilding the lily.

Again Big Daddy cleared his throat. "Cindy, what I'm

lookin' for is a ranch hand that can work side by side with my current ranch foreman, Montana here.''

"Oh?" She gave a mental shrug. After years of working alongside her brilliant father, she figured she could do that. Taking orders was nothing new.

Montana lifted his lazy gaze to her face, still deep in thought.

"We've interviewed more losers than we can shake a stick at this week, which is why I finally broke down and ran that ad, hopin' to weed out the culls. Now we are over-run with applicants, as you can see by the throng in the waitin' room. This job…'' Big Daddy pinched his wide, rubbery lips between his thumb and forefinger for a second and sighed. "This job is rough. Gotta work with a bunch of bonehead cowboys and hold your own. Takes a strong personality to do that." He chuckled and gestured to his silent nephew. "Like Montana here. He don't take no crap from nobody." He doffed his hat. "Pardon my French."

"I see."

"Plus, you gotta be able to string barbed wire, dig post holes, mend fences, fix broken gates, herd cattle, heft calves, feed livestock in bad weather, ride a horse all day, shoot the occasional rattler and abide the blistering sun."

"I can do that."

Big Daddy seemed not to hear. "We're also taking a real hard look at drought management. Been a big problem the last few years. Some of my outmost sections are downright deserts. Understanding irrigation, and maximizing water us-age would be a real plus. And, honey, Montana needs a strong right arm. Somebody with the right mix of temper-ament and machismo."

Sydney's heart began to sink. She was being dismissed, even before she had a chance to prove herself. She forced a mask of confidence, hoping to belie her sudden trepidation. "I can do that."

Montana's narrow gaze slowly roved from her face to her legs and settled at her ankles. Had she not needed this job so badly she'd have served him an ankle sandwich. However, on the outside chance that they might still hire her, she kept her feet planted firmly on the floor.

"Cindy, you are a very impressive young lady." Big Daddy tossed her folder onto a pile of what looked like hundreds of résumés. She knew right then and there that he would never take the time to peruse the documents she'd so carefully prepared. "We have quite a few more applicants to interview." He stood, signaling the end of the interview. "We'll get back to you with an answer within the next day or two."

Montana stood and extended his hand. "We've got your number." There was something in his tone that let Sydney know that he'd keep her number on file whether she got the job or not.

Rising from her chair, Sydney once again donned a dazzling smile and shook first Montana's hand, then his uncle's. "Thank you so much," she blathered, wanting nothing more than to get out of there and punch something, "for your time and consideration. I certainly look forward to hearing from you."

Big Daddy nodded. "Sure thing, Cindy."

"Sydney."

"Cindy."

Sydney sighed and left the office, shutting the door behind her. The dismal feeling that the news wouldn't be good when they did call escorted her out of the office, through the waiting room and into her broken-down truck. Defeated and depressed, Sydney forced her ailing engine to life and headed home.

* * *

"She was good."

"Real good."

"Best one yet."

"By far."

"Can't hire her."

"I figured you'd feel that way."

"Kinda like throwin' a hen in the fox coop."

Montana nodded. "Kind of." He probed the back of his neck with his fingertips. The muscles there were strung tighter than barbed wire. "Too bad."

"Don't I know it. You get a gander at the yahoos out there we still got to interview?"

Montana snorted. "I'm sure none of 'em could hold a candle to her. Hell, she's more qualified to run this place than we are."

"Yup."

"It would probably never work."

"Nah. Not someone that purty." Big Daddy gave his head a sad shake.

"Yeah. She was a looker." Her thick curly hair was the color of chestnuts. It had all been stuffed into a tidy bun, but Montana could imagine what it would look like flowing wild down her back. And those eyes. A piercing green gaze that could stop a heartbeat and get it chugging in reverse. Man. "She had a set of legs, didn't she?"

"Whoo, boy. And dainty little ankles. Made it hard not to stare."

"Sexual harassment suit waiting to happen."

"'Fraid so."

Montana wished he could make it work. Letting someone like her get away because of sexual politics would be a crying shame. He made another attempt to sway Big

Daddy. "She was an Aggie. Probably be used to getting the catcalls from the guys."

"True. A&M is a man's world. But this would be different, what with her livin' down in the bunkhouses with the guys and all. Too dangerous."

Exhaling heavily, Montana scanned the clipboard for the name of the next applicant. "Yeah. You're right. Too bad."

Chapter Two

Late the next afternoon Sydney watched as her neighbor, the aging Poppy Morton, shuffled into her kitchen, allowing the top part of her old-fashioned Dutch door to stay open. By the time Sydney got the door closed, a bothersome number of flies had followed him inside. She picked up a swatter and motioned for Poppy to take a seat at the kitchen table.

At one time, this room had been her late mother's dream kitchen. But now the faded daisy wallpaper was beginning to lose its grip on the wall and the ancient avocado and harvest-gold appliances were on their deathbeds.

"Don't move," she whispered after Poppy had settled his bony frame into the wooden chair.

His prickly cactus of a face stretched to reveal a set of snaggley teeth and a bulge of chewing tobacco. "Strike now and ya can get two."

"Not yet. There's one more." Sydney pursed her lips. "Timing is everything." She waited till all three flies were circling a crumb on the counter and went in for the kill.

Bingo. Satisfaction suffused her and she grinned and blew on the swatter as if it were the tip of a smoking gun. "Still got the touch."

"Yer the best," Poppy agreed, and raised his hand for a high five. Sydney smacked his palm and he grinned.

Poppy owned the spread next door and Sydney had grown up thinking of the old codger as an uncle. Since Poppy had become a widower and her own parents had passed on, they'd grown even closer. Once or twice a week, Sydney cooked dinner for the two of them. They'd talk ranching until one of them began to have trouble keeping their eyes open and then Poppy would mosey home.

After Sydney cleaned up the dead flies, she grabbed a chipped mug from one of the hooks under the cupboard, poured him a cup of coffee and freshened her own cup.

"So, I just come over to find out how it went yesterday. Didja get the job?"

"Well," Sydney said on a beleaguered exhale, "that's a good question." She took the seat opposite and regarded his sweet, time-weathered face.

"They musta liked ya."

"Oh." Sydney thought back to Montana's gaze, riveted to her legs as she'd exited the office. "I think they liked me well enough. Whether or not they'll hire me is a different story."

"I don't know why not. You got more goin' for ya than most men twice yer age."

"Be that as it may, I had the funniest feeling that they were trying to tell me that the job would go to a man."

Poppy was indignant. "Why, that's not fair." His sensitive streak was a mile wide.

"Fair or not, it's still a fact of life."

Poppy harrumphed. "When are they gonna call ya?"

"Said they'd call within a day or two. I'll probably never hear from them again."

"So whater ya gonna do now?"

'I just don't know. I'm running out of options. I thought the sale of my livestock would bring in a lot more money, but the doggone market is so soft."

"Yup. Practically gave that prize bull of yers away."

"Couldn't be helped. If I'm ever going to pay off the debt that Daddy left, I have to unload everything that's not nailed down." She held up her coffee mug and grinned. "Want to buy a cup? I'll give it to you cheap, what with the crack and all."

"You know I'd help ya if I could, darlin'." Poppy reached behind his chair, opened the door under the sink and grabbed the garbage pail, for use as a spittoon. "Bless yer daddy's heart. He was a miracle worker with animals, but he wasn't much on business. Although, to his credit, it took him longer to run this place into the ground than most."

"Now, there's a compliment."

A stream of tobacco juice landed in the pail and Poppy blotted his lips on the back of his sleeve. "You get any nibbles on that ad you ran to board horses?"

"Mmm-hmm. Got a call yesterday. I can rent out half a dozen stalls right away, maybe more by the end of the month. But renting stalls and leasing pasture still won't bring in enough to save this place. I have to get a job. Pure and simple. A good job. With decent pay. Better than decent pay."

Lord knew she'd applied for every available job in the College Station, Bryan and Hidden Valley areas. Most of the jobs were menial labor and wouldn't cover the bills. Sydney snagged a napkin from the holder on the table and put it under her mug to soak up the ring. Jobs that utilized her unique combination of skills were simply not available at the moment. Unless she counted the Brubaker job.

As if his thoughts were traveling the same path as her own, Poppy said, "I have a feeling that Circle BO job will happen for you. They ain't gonna care that you're a woman. You got the talent and energy of a whole crew of ranch hands."

"Wouldn't that be great? The ad said excellent wage and benefits."

"Them Brubakers sure are rich. Probably don't think twice about throwin' a ton of money at the right person for the job."

"I don't know about that. Things haven't changed much over the years. Even on the bigger ranches, the hands still don't pull down very good wages. Unless they're related to the family, I suppose."

"Now, don't be thinkin' all negative. I'd bet them Brubakers would have to pay more than you'd make waiting tables down at Ned's Lonestar Grill or pumping gas at the Get & Go, don't you think?"

"I hope so. I've got years to pay on the loan at the rate I'm going."

"Honey, if anyone can do it, you can. You got yer mama's pluck. Listen, if ya get the job, I'll keep an eye on your spread for as long as ya need."

"You're a peach, Poppy." Not that there was all that much to keep an eye on anymore. A few barn cats were all the "livestock" she owned.

The phone on the wall jangled.

Sydney bit her lower lip. "That might be them."

It rang again.

And then, once again.

"You gonna answer that?"

"I'm scared."

"Why? Yer the best dern candidate for the job. Pick up the blasted phone and tell 'em you can start in the morning."

Sydney grinned. With the exception of his bowed legs and grizzled features, Poppy was a regular cheerleader.

"Okay." She stood and answered the phone. "Hello?"

"Cindy MacKenzie, please." Immediately she recognized Montana's distinctive baritone. She signaled to Poppy that this was it. Poppy gripped the edge of the table and leaned toward her.

"This is she," she replied, not bothering to correct his mispronunciation of her first name.

"Oh. Hi. Montana Brubaker here." There was a quality to his tone that had her pulse quickening. Was he calling with good news?

"Listen. I just called to let you know that the position that you applied for has been…er…closed. I'm really sorry. You seem to have a lot going for you and I know that you'll find the perfect job to fit your skills."

Unbidden, tears sprang to Sydney's eyes and a lump lodged in her throat. "Oh…I…oh." She hated how breathy and devastated her voice sounded, but for the life of her, she couldn't put two coherent words together. It both amazed and maddened her that she'd allowed herself to pin so much hope on this job. It was just that she was so perfectly qualified. She wound the telephone cord around her fingers and struggled to swallow her disappointment.

"We will definitely keep your résumé on file," Montana continued, his voice soothing, his demeanor contrite, "and if there is any way we can find a spot for you in the future, we'll do it."

"Oh. I… Okay."

"Thanks again for taking the time to come in and interview. It was really nice meeting you."

"Oh. Thank you," Sydney said, wanting to slam down the phone and throw a tantrum. She thought about pressing for reasons that they had passed on her, but decided not to bother. She knew it was because she was a woman.

When she expected him to hang up, Montana lingered on the line. "Big Daddy was very impressed. As was I."

Big deal. She was still no closer to having a job. "Thank you," she murmured and blinked back the ridiculous tears that threatened.

As if sensing that she was having a difficult time, Poppy reached out and patted her hand. This small gesture gave her courage. Sydney took a steadying breath.

"Uh, before you go...the ad in the paper didn't mention the salary range. Would that be public information?"

Poppy winked at her as Montana quoted figures that far exceeded her wildest dreams. Her face crumpled as she thought of what this money could have meant for her ranch. "Ah. Well. Thank you for the information. And for calling to let me know."

After she'd bid Montana goodbye, she sagged into her chair and bit back a sob.

Poppy pulled a handkerchief from his back pocket and laid it on the table in front of her.

"I didn't get the job."

"I figured. Their loss."

"They didn't even *look* at my résumé."

"Sexist pigs," Poppy muttered around another stream of tobacco juice.

"It's not fair. You should have seen the other candidates for the job. Drunks, bums, perverts, every one."

"You find out which one of these guys they hired?"

"No. He didn't say. In fact—" Sydney frowned "—it was a little strange, the way he phrased it. Said the job was closed. Didn't say the position was filled. Closed. Not filled.''

"Big difference." Poppy's wiry brows knitted.

Suddenly madder than a wet hornet, Sydney scraped back her chair and stepped to the phone. Savagely she put the old rotary dial through its paces, dialing the number she'd memorized for the Brubaker ranch offices.

When the secretary answered, Sydney noisily cleared her throat and lowered her voice a couple of octaves. "Hello, my name is…ah…Syd. Syd…Mac and I'm calling to find out if the ranch hand job I saw in the Sunday paper is still available."

"One moment." Hold music serenaded her as she was transferred. The line was picked up on the first ring. "Circle BO. Montana speaking."

"Ah heh ah, hem. Syd Mac here. Just wondering if the ranch hand job I saw in Sunday's paper is still available."

"Yes, Mr. Mac. We are still interviewing for that position."

As Montana went into his I-need-a-right-hand-man spiel, Sydney clapped her hand over the mouthpiece and shot an indignant look at Poppy. "They're still interviewing!" she hissed.

"The chauvinists! You oughta sue 'em."

She rolled her eyes. "Where would I get money for a lawyer?"

Montana's mellifluous voice tickled her ear. "Mr. Mac, would you like to talk to my secretary about putting your name on the list for an interview?"

"I…uh…"

Sydney froze.

A second shot at an interview? Was that possible? Just because over the phone she passed as a male? A wild thought, born of desperation, began to take shape in her mind's eye. Should she interview as a male? She'd fooled him on the phone. Could she do it in person? She wasn't all that busty. Surely with the right clothes she could pass as a wiry boy. The handsome wage that he'd mentioned echoed in her mind. Fear of losing the ranch that had been in her family for generations spurred her on.

"Yes," she barked in the most macho fashion she could affect. "Do that." When the secretary came back on, Sydney said, "Honey, put me down for an interview tomorrow afternoon, if you have a slot open." Slack jawed, Poppy stared as she made the appointment.

"Will 2:00 p.m. work for you, sir?" came the secretary's polite inquiry.

"Great—2:00 p.m. is fine."

"And your last name again?"

"Mac."

"Thank you for calling the Circle BO, Mr. Mac. We'll see you tomorrow at two."

Two o'clock the following day found Sydney seated once again in the waiting room of the Brubaker ranch offices. This time, however, no one was leering at her legs. Due, no doubt, to the fact that today she was sporting a pair of calfskin cowboy boots from her rodeo days, a pair of 501 jeans, a faded denim Western shirt and a leather vest. A sports bra smashed her more feminine attributes and a Stetson was clapped over the top of her newly shorn and dyed dark brown locks.

That had been the hardest part of this whole deal. Cutting her crowning glory. Poppy had told her she looked like G.I. Jane, which was a compliment, coming from him, as Poppy liked women who kicked butt. Besides, she'd be able to pay a few bills with the sale of her hair to a local wig maker. So, even if she didn't get the job this go round, it wasn't a total loss. Still, the stubble at the back of her head felt strange.

The second hardest part had been the chewing tobacco. How Poppy kept from retching with all that tingly, gritty, distasteful mush floating around in his mouth, she'd never know. They'd practiced all evening, and she never did get the hang of spitting. Just dribbled and drooled and fought her gag reflex. Poppy assured her that practice made perfect.

She'd decided to forgo that stuff for the interview. Made it too hard to talk. And talking like a man would be hard enough.

As she perused her new and decidedly more macho résumé, she adjusted her dark glasses on her nose. The less face she showed, the better, she figured. There was a speck of polish still left on one of her newly clipped nails and she hurriedly gnawed it off.

A feeling of déjà vu crept over her as the door to the inner offices opened and Montana Brubaker stepped outside, closing the door behind him.

Showtime. Her ears began to ring, her pulse skipped several important beats. She yanked her nail out of her mouth.

"Mac?"

"Yo," Sydney answered and stood. Again, all eyes of the latest motley crew seated nearby watched her cross the room. Using a rangy gait she'd practiced all morning, she ambled over to him and, taking his extended hand, gave it a bone-crushing squeeze.

His eyes widened imperceptibly and when she let go, he rubbed his hand a little to ease the pain. Next time, Sydney thought sheepishly, she'd have to go a little easier on the handshake. But she was new at this stuff. It would take a while to get the hang of being male, she was sure.

"Mr. Mac?" This time there was no flash of annoyance behind his warm smile.

"Syd."

"Syd, then. Hi. Nice to meet you. I'm Montana Brubaker." He paused and studied Sydney for a moment. "Have we met before? You seem familiar to me."

Sydney's heart began to hammer against her ribs. "No."

"You sure?" His gaze traveled over her features as Sydney ducked her head and coughed. "I have the funniest feeling that we've met somewhere before."

"I don't think so."

He shook his head. "Never mind. It'll come to me."

Sydney hoped not.

The door to the office stayed closed and Montana made no move to enter and begin the interviewing process, as he had last time. Instead, he stepped over to his secretary's desk and gave her a flirtatious grin that brought out the dimples Sydney remembered so well from their first meeting. Golly, he was handsome. Looked to be in his late twenties or early thirties. Idly, Sydney wondered if he was married.

Montana handed the secretary his clipboard.

"BettyJean." He lowered his voice in a confidential manner and Sydney had to strain to catch every word. "I've got to go up to Dallas for an auction and I'll be gone overnight. Big Daddy's gonna handle the rest of today's interviews for the ranch hand position."

Lowering her husky voice to match his intimate quality, BettyJean cooed, "Ooo, an auction sounds like fun." She tossed her platinum hair over her shoulder and stretched her sweater across her ample curves. "Wish I could go with you."

"Nah. You'd be too distracting."

"Oh, pooh." BettyJean giggled, then sobering, whispered so that Sydney had to take a nonchalant step toward them to hear better. "I know you never go out anymore because you're still nursing a broken heart after what that awful Delle did to you."

"BettyJean, someday you're going to have to tell us how you really felt about Delle," Montana teased.

Delle? Who was Delle? BettyJean's interest, coupled with his ringless finger, told Sydney that Montana was single. Not that she cared one way or the other, of course. She was simply curious.

BettyJean pouted prettily. "I sensed that Delle was a con artist from the beginning. Could see right through her, I could," she declared.

Quickly Sydney took a step back and let Montana shield her from BettyJean's apparent psychic abilities.

"Well, we can discuss this another time." His tone didn't seem all that enthusiastic to Sydney, but that didn't daunt BettyJean.

"Over dinner?"

"Whatever." He checked his watch. "Hey, I gotta go. I got my cell phone with me and my pager, too. Let me know if anything earthshaking happens this afternoon. Otherwise, I'll see you tomorrow."

"Bye," BettyJean breathed.

Montana winked.

Sydney felt invisible. Worse yet, like an invisible boy. Which, she supposed, was good, all things considered.

She stood there, wondering what to do next.

Remembering Sydney, Montana turned around. "Oh. Hey, Syd, I'm sorry, guy, but I won't be able to stay for the interview. Instead, my uncle, Big Daddy Brubaker, will be talking to you today. I'll look forward to hearing Big Daddy's report tomorrow morning."

If Sydney was disappointed that she wouldn't have a

chance to put old Montana in his place this afternoon, she was also kind of relieved that he would not be there. One less Brubaker to convince that she was the man for the job was all right with her. She looked into his eyes from behind the safety of her tinted lenses. Surely his piercing gaze would undo her bravado. Undermine her ability to focus.

Something about the way he was looking at her now unnerved her.

"It'll come to me," he muttered under his breath. For a second, it appeared as if he was going to extend his hand once again, but then, thinking better of it, he gestured to the office door instead. "Go on inside, Syd. Big Daddy is waiting for you." Then he addressed the rest of the men waiting in the lobby. "Good luck to all of you and thank you for your interest in working for the Circle BO."

As Sydney watched him spin on his heel and walk away, she made mental notes of his masculine carriage and the sheer animal magnetism he exuded. Boy howdy, he was impressive. Her gaze slid to BettyJean's longing expression. Apparently she was not the only one who thought so.

Sydney sighed. The man was dangerous. Being his assistant might be a little more daunting than she'd originally thought. Although her being a boy and all would surely simplify things.

He blew past the large glass doors and suddenly the lights seemed to dim. When Montana Brubaker left a room, everyone knew it. He was exactly the kind of man she should emulate for this interview, she decided. Strong. Tough. Fearless.

Okay, strong and tough, anyway. The butterflies in her stomach fluttered as nervous energy played havoc with her confidence. Like she did just before a barrel race, Sydney took a few deep, cleansing breaths to calm her fears. She could do this. She had to. Not just for her ranch, but for all womankind.

"Good luck, darlin'," BettyJean whispered, and winked at Sydney.

"Uh…" Nonplussed, Sydney backed toward the office door. "Uh…thanks, ma'am."

Just as she had done two days prior, Sydney strode into the office and greeted the effusive Big Daddy Brubaker. Even though he had overlooked her because of a stupid prejudice, there was something infinitely likable about the wizened elf of a man. Something genuine. Loving. Sydney couldn't put her finger on it, but he exuded something that was evident in his nephew, as well. A quality that inspired trust.

However, this darling old man and his gorgeous nephew were—as Poppy had so eloquently phrased it—sexist pigs.

She had to keep that in mind, or this would never work.

After they shook hands, Sydney dropped into the same club chair she'd used last time. Spreading her legs, the way she'd seen Montana do, she propped her elbows on her knees and let her hands dangle.

"Mr. Brubaker—" No, that wasn't low enough, she decided, and tried again. "Ahhh, heh heh hem, Mr. Brubaker, I brought a résumé but I'd rather just tell you about myself, if it's okay with you. I find paper so impersonal."

Big Daddy beamed. "That's my motto."

"Good. Well, let me start by telling you that I grew up on a ranch as a young…ster. Worked side by side with my daddy as his strong right arm." Sydney sprawled back in her chair and guffawed. "Lucky for us, I had the right mix of temperament and machismo for the job." She sobered and jutted her jaw, doing her best to appear masterful. "Most of our days were spent stringing barbed wire, digging post holes, mending fences, fixing broken gates, herding cattle, hefting calves, feeding livestock in lousy weather, riding horses all day in the hot Texas sun...you know the drill.''

Big Daddy's jaw sagged.

''By the way, drought management happens to be a specialty of mine. Show me an irrigation system and I'll show you a way to improve it.'' Feeling blustery and full of vinegar, Sydney barreled on. ''I've done the rodeo circuit, dabbled in large animal veterinary medicine and worked as crew boss on two different ranches.'' Okay, she thought, that was stretching it, calling Poppy a crew, but she had worked on his spread as well as her own, for a grand total of two. And Poppy didn't mind being bossed around. ''I'm decent to work with, easygoing, but I don't take no crap off anybody. Except for my boss, sir.

''I have a way with animals that I inherited from my daddy. I can rope and brand and target shoot and play poker with the best of 'em. I'd be glad to show you if you've got a horse, a gun and a deck of cards I can borrow.''

Her grin was so cocky, she was sure that any moment now, Big Daddy was going to call her on this laughable charade. Here she was, barely taller than this millionaire munchkin. And though she had good muscle tone, she made a pretty scrawny man. This ruse was so absurd, surely she'd be found out and kicked off this property any minute now. Until then, however, she figured she might as well teach a couple of good old boys a lesson or two about how to treat a lady.

''When can you start?''

Sydney stared at Big Daddy's lips. ''Pardon?''

''When can you start, son?''

Start what? Target shooting and playing poker? Surely he couldn't be referring to the job.

"Right now," she blustered, figuring she'd catch his drift in a minute.

"Tomorrow will be soon enough, boy." Big Daddy grinned. "I don't have to talk to ya all day to get the feeling that you will be the perfect sidekick for my nephew."

"You don't? You do? I... Thank you." Sydney gulped. She'd been so busy daydreaming about the salary, it hadn't really dawned on her that she'd be spending a great deal of her time working side by side with the rugged Montana.

"I'll give you sixty days probation and if Montana likes you...you're permanent. Deal?"

Sydney nodded. *If Montana likes her?* Her eyes drifted to a framed photograph of Montana on the shelves behind Big Daddy. In this picture, he was wearing a tux and posing with a wedding party. His brother's wedding, if their incredible resemblance meant anything.

Big Daddy followed her gaze. "Yeah. That's Montana. At his brother Dakota's weddin' to Elizabeth. We're gonna miss havin' Dakota workin' out here as ranch foreman, but Montana is just as good. Dakota's taken a CEO position in one of his daddy's companies. I make all my sons and nephews—" he gestured to another picture of a large group of men "—work the ranch after college until they're about thirty and are ready to run off and head up a corporation. Makes men out of 'em. But then, I'm always losin' a good foreman, and that's a huge job out here. Montana will be thrilled to have you on board. And since you're so young, you can stay on for years, helping smooth the transition between each future foreman."

Years? Oh, good heavens. "Yess..." Sydney coughed and lowered her voice. "Yessir."

"You feeling okay, boy?"

"Great, sir."

"Good. Can't have you gettin' sick on your first day.

Our little gal BettyJean, out front, will have you fill out all the paperwork and such, then you run home and pack what you need to get settled into the bunkhouse tomorrow morning. We provide your housing. We like to have our hands livin' close by, in case we need 'em in an emergency. We provide little two-man bunkhouses. They're simple little two-bedroom, one-bath units, but they're nice. Living on the ranch is no problem for you, is it?''

"No, sir."

"Good. That's what I like to hear."

If that's what Big Daddy liked, that's what Big Daddy got. Sydney needed the paycheck he was offering too much to quibble. Besides, the commute from Hidden Valley to College Station was well over an hour. Living here would save her precious gas money and wear and tear on her old truck. Poppy had said he'd hold down her fort. She could drive out to her place on her days off and do whatever chores needed doing.

"Good, good. Since Dakota moved out last month, we got a spare room in Montana's place. You'll bunk with him. That'll work perfect, as he'll be spending all his time trainin' you at first anyway."

Sydney gaped at Big Daddy. *She had to live with Montana?* Her heart sank like a stone. How on earth could she keep up this ruse if she had to bunk with the boss?

Early the next morning Montana took a seat across from his uncle's desk in the main ranch office. "BettyJean tells me you hired some new hotshot while I was gone yesterday."

"Yeah!" Delighted, Big Daddy pulled a celebratory cigar from his vest pocket. With a snick of his lighter, the room was suddenly filled with the rich aroma of one of

Cuba's finest cigars. "You're gonna love him, boy! This kid is everything we've been lookin' for and more."

"Sounds too good to be true."

"I thought so, too. 'At's why I hired him, right on the spot. Didn't bother checkin' references or anything. Told him he got sixty days probation and if he didn't work out, he was history." Big Daddy blew a smoke ring, then with great expertise, blew another through the middle. "Only drawback I could see is his age. I didn't ask, but he looks young. Voice is still a little rough around the edges. Still, I think he'll earn the men's respect. Seems like the kind of guy who can hold his own."

"What's his name?"

"Syd Mac."

"Right. Right." Montana squinted out the window. "I know who you're talking about. Met him on the way out the door yesterday. A little runt of a guy. So he's my new assistant, huh?"

Big Daddy harrumphed. "Bein' small of stature don't need to hold ya back, if yer a real man."

Montana chuckled. "I suppose you're right. So where is he?"

"Said he'd be here at eight this morning, so I imagine he'll be here any sec…. Why, speak of the devil. Syd. Come on in, boy. Meet your new boss."

Sydney stepped into the room and stood shuffling awkwardly by the door. "Hello."

Again, that overpowering feeling of familiarity washed over Montana. He knew he knew this guy from somewhere, and until he figured it out, it was going to drive him crazy.

"Come on, and take a load off, Syd," Big Daddy ordered, and gestured to one of the two club chairs in front of his desk. He motioned for his nephew to take the other.

"Montana tells me you two met on his way out the door yesterday."

The kid nodded and Montana knew that he'd met this guy other than on his way out the door. And it was recently. In fact, it was right here in this room. In that very chair. Montana studied Syd's rather delicate profile. Professional cowboys with those gamin features were rare indeed.

Unless...

Montana leaned slightly forward.

Unless the cowboy in question was a...cow*girl*.

Why, that little stinker. He narrowed his eyes as a grim smile stole across his lips. The kid was that hotshot redhead with the legs that went on forever.

Syd Mac was Cindy MacKenzie!

Chapter Three

As Syd and Big Daddy conversed, Montana decided to keep his rather startling revelation to himself. For the time being, anyway.

He'd have a little fun with this, for a while, before he fired Miss Cindy MacKenzie's shapely little butt. And he would fire her. No doubt about that. Montana Brubaker did not take kindly to being conned. Not even by a beautiful woman. Especially by a beautiful woman.

He was still reeling from Delle's betrayal.

Fingers tented under his chin, Montana propped his elbows on the armrests of his chair and stared at Syd. A small smile played at the corners of his mouth. He could tell he was unnerving her, by the way she stammered and stuttered as she spoke with Big Daddy.

"Got the first-day jitters, boy?" Big Daddy wondered with a laugh.

"I guess so, sir." Syd nodded.

"Well then, have a cigar. They always relax me." Big Daddy flipped up the lid and offered the box.

Sydney darted a quick look at Montana.

Stifling a grin, Montana angled his head in an encouraging manner. "Go ahead. They're about the best you'll find."

"Mmm." Syd squinted, and made her choice as if she were selecting a chocolate.

Montana followed suit and noticed how she copied the way he removed the band and the cellophane. He could tell she was trying to look unfazed as he bit off the end and blew it into a nearby trash can. Like a dog with a bone, Syd worried the tip of her cigar for a while and, when her mouth was sufficiently filled with tobacco, he offered her a light. He could tell she was miserable as the smoke curled into her eyes and closed off her throat.

Montana leaned back and enjoyed his cigar. And the moment. Yeah. He hadn't had this much fun in months.

Yep, yep, yep. If she thought she could do the job of a man on this ranch, she was wrong. He'd give her enough rope to hang herself, and then he'd can her. Send her packing. Give her the boot.

Montana frowned. If he didn't know better, he'd be tempted to think he had some unresolved issues when it came to Delle.

Nah. A con artist got what a con artist deserved.

"You got your stuff with you today, son?" Big Daddy asked, seemingly oblivious to everything.

"Yes, sir. I can move in anytime."

"Montana, after this little meetin', why don't you give Syd a tour of his new digs and give him a hand moving in."

"My pleasure."

As Big Daddy and Syd hammered out the typical new-guy details, Montana found it hard to believe that Big Daddy didn't realize that Syd was Cindy. The old man's eyesight had to be failing him. It was so obvious that she was female.

It was going to be real interesting, sharing a cabin with her. Too bad about her hair, he mused, thinking back to her long, sexy auburn tresses. Her hair was shorter than his was now, and a rather boring shade of brown. Not that she wouldn't look dynamite either way given the right miniskirt and some lipstick, but if he had his druthers, he preferred the long, shiny auburn hair.

Moot point now, he figured, being that she wasn't going to be hanging around all that long.

When Big Daddy had finally given Syd the rundown on the employee policies and they'd all stubbed out their cigars, Montana reached out and none too gently clapped Syd on the back, then, gripping her by the shoulder, rocked her back and forth.

"Good to have you on board, Syd," Montana said and stood. "Come on with me, and I'll give you the nickel tour of our place."

He knew.

Something about the way Montana looked at her made Sydney nearly certain that the jig was up. Yes. He must know.

Didn't he?

Then again, maybe not.

How could he know? After all, Big Daddy didn't seem to suspect a thing. And Poppy had told her she looked pretty tough. But he'd been laughing pretty hard when he'd said it.

Dizzy with panic, she struggled to keep up with Montana's lanky stride. As they barreled along, he led her from the ranch offices to a small grouping of cabins that lay under the shade of a thick stand of willows and live oaks.

Surely, she lamented, huffing as she trotted beside him, keeping up this ruse would be the death of her. With a sideways glance, she tried to gauge the meaning of the enigmatic expression that lurked behind Montana's blue eyes.

He was such a hard duck to lead.

That was it.

Of course. She was simply reading him wrong. She was jumping to conclusions because she was scared. He probably didn't have any idea she was the woman he knew as Cindy. He certainly wasn't treating her like a lady. Maybe he stared at everyone this way. Maybe she should stop worrying so much, and be thankful for the opportunity to prove herself worthy of this job.

A good-sized pond, situated in the center of this backwoods neighborhood for cowboys, reflected a deep, sea-blue summer sky through which cottony clouds silently floated over the Brubakers' endless ranch. The cabins were reminiscent of the type found at most summer camps—rustic yet homey, simple yet sturdy. Small yet…intimate.

It was heaven. And hell.

She glanced at Montana as he pointed out the highlights they passed.

"This here is Fuzzy and Red's duplex. They've worked here the longest, so they each get their own place. Over there is Hunt and Colt's bunk. Big Daddy's son—and my cousin—Kenny rooms with my brother Tex in that one, and next door are Big Daddy's other sons, the twins, Waylon and Willie. Our place is down here at the very end." He indicated a tiny cabin that, under other circumstances, Sydney would have found romantic.

"Great," she barked, and then, for good measure, she spit into the bushes, the way Poppy had advised her to do from time to time. The way she knew a real man would.

She wasn't really sure why men felt compelled to dampen the foliage that way. Must be a territorial thing.

Her gaze shifted to the area behind the cabins. Off in the distance, a slight breeze rippled through vast oceans of grain. Long-horned, cud-chewing bovine herds bawled and churned up dust as they were being moved from pasture to pasture by the men who were undoubtedly her new neighbors. She longed to join them.

"Where'd you park?"

Montana's voice snapped her back to the present.

"Over there." She pointed to the parking area near the main office, where her dilapidated truck sat loaded with a few boxes of her worldly goods.

"Okay, you can pull your truck up front and unload your stuff after I show you around."

"Okay."

She bounded up the porch stairs and followed him into what appeared to be a kitchen-dining-living-room combo. The TV/conversation area contained a nondescript sofa covered with an Indian print blanket. An old trunk served as a coffee table. Two comfy-looking recliners flanked the opposite side. In the dining nook, a wooden table and four chairs were sitting in front of a sliding glass door that led to a decent-sized deck. The galley kitchen, though sparse, seemed to have all the necessary equipment. It was certainly more modern than her own. All in all, it was surprisingly homey.

"We can take turns cooking," Montana said. "I make a mean pot of chili."

"Mmm." Sydney hated chili.

"Back this way are the bedrooms. Mine's on the left, yours is on the right." He spoke to her over his shoulder as he led her down a short hallway. Situated at the end of

CAROLYN ZANE 41

this hall and separating the two bedrooms was the one and only bathroom.

"Sorry about the bathroom door. Before Dakota got married, some of the guys got to horsing around at his bachelor party, and it fell off. I've been meaning to get it fixed, but I just haven't gotten to it." Montana turned and grinned at her. "Not that it's that big of a deal, us being guys and all, right?"

Strangled laughter bubbled past Sydney's lips. "Right." Oh, good grief. How the devil was she supposed to do her daily business with no bathroom door? She made a mental note to fix the door the first free moment she got.

"Come on, I'll show you where you sleep." He hustled Sydney to the right. His arm swept the masculine room, simply furnished with bookshelves laden with rodeo trophies and framed fishing pictures of the Brubaker boys and their catches. The hardwood floors were bare except for a few scatter rugs, and the knotty pine walls were adorned with the stuffed heads of several wild animals, the most prominent being the moose that was mounted over the bed.

"I shot that guy," Montana boasted, "on a hunting trip to Alaska."

"Nice," Sydney said, hating its glassy-eyed stare. She was sure it would give her nightmares.

"This was my old room. I shifted over to Dakota's after he got married. It's bigger." He grinned. "Rank."

"That's cool." She didn't care, just as long as her room had a door. It did.

"How old are you?"

The question stymied her, coming from left field. "I'm…" For a nanosecond she hesitated. How old should she be? How old did he want her to be? Confessing that she was twenty-eight with her high voice and lack of beard would surely lead to suspicion. The ad had said "must be eighteen" to apply. "Eighteen, sir."

"And your voice is still changing, huh?"

"Late bloomer, sir."

"Stop calling me sir. Makes me feel old. Call me Montana."

"Yes, sir. Uh…Montana."

"That's better. Well, don't just stand there, kid. Go pull your rig around and get unloaded. I've got some work to do in the office. When you're done, come get me, and I'll take you out and show you the ropes. When we get back, I'll introduce you to the guys."

Because she wanted to make a good first impression, Sydney quickly unpacked the few boxes she'd brought, and headed to the office to meet Montana. Unpacking had been a cinch, as she no longer had any need for a blow-dryer or any of the hair rigmarole that would usually take up an entire suitcase by itself. She longed for her feminine creature comforts, her familiar nighty, her lacy underthings, her favorite perfume. However, she figured she could indulge in a little nail polish and some eye makeup on her days off, when she went home to check on things.

In spite of her promptness, Montana kept her waiting for a half hour, while the silly BettyJean attempted to flirt with her. Sydney played dumb and shy and eventually BettyJean gave up. When Montana finally emerged from the office, he whistled for her as if she were a dog and then strode out of the glass double doors with that infuriatingly easy male gait of his, and didn't even check to see if she was following.

When they reached the stables, Montana introduced her to her horse, Geranium, fitted her with a saddle from the massive tack room and then let her ready her mount while he saddled his own horse, Bullet.

They left the paddock on a road that stretched over the horizon, where the crystal-clear blue of the Texas sky met the golden waves of an endless sea of grass. For what seemed like miles they cantered along, gliding down the road, which appeared to lead nowhere in particular. The acreage that made up Big Daddy's range was breathtaking.

Geranium was a sensitive steed, Sydney noted, obeying every nuance of even her imagined commands. Someone with a marvelous touch had nurtured and broken this horse. Already, she was in love.

With ease, Geranium crested a steep rise, barely laboring, even after having traveled so far. The sun was now high in the sky, leaving behind its seat on the eastern horizon. Warm rays relaxed Sydney, giving her a sense of calm and control she hadn't enjoyed since arriving on this land.

"See that little silver ribbon running through the stand of trees in that gully?" Montana asked as he reined in his mount.

Sydney rode up next to him and followed his gaze with her own. She nodded.

"That's the main irrigation stream for the sections on this side of the ranch. It feeds the livestock tanks as well as supplying some of the water for the crops. As you might guess, we have had to be extremely careful with our water supplies over the past few years. Lost some cattle and grass crops due to drought. We're working on never letting that happen again."

"How far does that stream run?"

"'Bout as far as the eye can see. Big Daddy's got about ten thousand acres of prime ranch." There was no boasting in his tone. Simply the facts, simply stated. "The land is cattle and grazing pasture mostly. Some hay and grain

fields in the back sections.'' He gestured in the opposite
direction to a field of oil pump jacks off in the distance.
''Those sections out there are full of rocking horses. But
those are only some of Big Daddy's oil fields. The rest of
'em are scattered around the state. He and my daddy own
some in Oklahoma, too.''

''Mmm.'' What Sydney wouldn't give for a single rocking horse on her land. It would certainly make paying her
debts a cinch.

They rode for another hour and only saw the merest tip
of the ranch iceberg. It was awesome. And though Sydney
had the education and experience to run her place, she was
sure that working here would be an invaluable addition to
her knowledge. Cutting her hair and coming to work here
had been the right thing to do, she was sure now.

''Come on, kid.'' Around noon, Montana finally reined
his horse around and headed back down the road toward
the stables. ''You can see the rest of this place another time.
Let's go meet the guys.''

Her brief elation faded. The guys. All of the calm she'd
been enjoying suddenly evaporated. ''Great,'' she asserted
as manfully as she knew how, and only hoped her trepidation didn't show.

When they arrived back at the paddock, a number of the
regular hands were there and eager to meet Syd. After he
and Syd had dismounted, Montana made introductions,
watching closely to gauge the guys' reaction to the new
kid. Like Big Daddy, they didn't seem to notice that Syd
was not all he was cracked up to be.

Beat the hell out of Montana.

To him, it was so obvious that she was a woman. Were
they all blind? Or did he notice the difference because he'd
met her as a woman to begin with? He couldn't figure it

out. The delicate features. The small hands. The shapely hips. It all screamed woman to him.

He called to his brother, "Tex, put the horses up, will you? And take Syd with you. Show him around." Montana waved them off and signaled one of the older hands. "Fuzzy, come on over here for a second, will you?" He leaned up against the split rail fence and crossed his ankles.

"Whatcha need, boss?"

"Just wondered what your impression of the new guy is."

Fuzzy shifted the straw in his mouth from one corner to the other. "Seems like an upright kind of guy. True, he hasn't been around the block too many times, but I think he'll settle in, once he gets the hang of the way we do things around here. I hear tell he's a real hotshot."

"You don't notice anything...different about the kid?"

Frowning, Fuzzy gave his head a thoughtful shake. "Nah. Not really. Why do you ask?"

"I don't know." Montana looked into the main stable to watch Tex and Syd unsaddle the horses and cart the gear back to the tack room. Montana could hear Tex give casual instruction about the daily routine, and Syd respond with intelligent questions. If Tex thought Syd was unusual in any respect, he didn't let on. Montana shifted his gaze to Fuzzy. "Don't you think he's a little...oh...I don't know...wimpy?"

Fuzzy squinted off into the shadowed interior. "Well, he ain't the biggest hand we ever had, and he sounds like a real kid, what with that squeaky voice of his, but he's young yet. Give him a chance, boss. He's got sixty days. If you don't like him, you can deal with him then."

Montana grunted. So. Cindy already had the guys converting to her camp. Fine. Eventually, everything would all come out in the wash. Conniving women always got theirs.

"Hey, Montana," Tex hollered.

"Yeah?" He pushed off the split rails and crossed the paddock. Entering through the stable's giant double doors, Montana blinked and let his eyes adjust to the sudden dimness, then moved down the broad hallway to the tack room. There, a few more of the hands had gathered and were introducing themselves to the new kid and making small talk.

"Some of us were thinking about going down to Jubilee's tonight for a few beers and some ribs."

"A first-day-on-the-job party." Colt grinned.

Montana rolled his eyes. "You yahoos don't need any excuse to party."

Tex laughed and jostled Syd. "He's right. But you'll find that out about us soon enough, kid. We do love to paint the town red. You look like a rabble-rouser yourself."

Montana glanced at Syd.

"Oh, you know it." She plucked a straw from a bale and poked it into the corner of her mouth. "I'm a partying fool."

"Great, then. You'll fit right in," Tex said. "Don't make any plans for the last Friday of each month, either. Usually a bunch of us will go into town and hit on women. You'll love it."

Syd looked as if she might swallow her straw. "Ohhh. Okay. Sure. Whatever."

Montana coughed to cover the burst of belly laughter he felt building. He'd have to jot that on his calendar. Watching Syd pick up women with the guys was something he wouldn't miss for anything.

"What about tonight, boss? You want to go to Jubilee's with us?"

"You bet." Montana could tell Syd was doing her best to hide her misery at the thought of dinner at the truck stop with the guys tonight and—later in the month—an evening of wine, women and song. He grinned and clapped her on the shoulder. "Sounds like a great idea. Just the way to welcome the kid into our fold. What do you say, Syd? Tonight? Ribs and beer on me."

"Okay. Sounds…great."

Great. This was just…great.

"Isn't this great, kid?" Montana scooted into the giant shiny black Naugahyde booth after Sydney and settled in right up against her. "You gotta love it."

"Ohhh, yeah. Love it." Her smile frozen to her face, Syd sat wedged between Fuzzy and Montana. Colt, Kenny, Red, Tex and Willie crammed in behind them, to make up the rest of the horseshoe-shaped seating arrangement. Jostling and laughing, they all seemed to be the best of buddies and having the time of their lives.

"Best ribs in Texas, right here. Sauce all over your face and hands," Montana grinned. "You don't just eat 'em. You wear 'em home."

"Gosh. That sounds so…so…" Sydney groped for the proper response and finally just gave up. It was so noisy here it didn't really make any difference. A mediocre country-western band played, and what they lacked in talent, they made up for in enthusiasm.

The Jubilee Rib-O-Rama at the truck stop where the interstate exited to Hidden Valley had never been high on Sydney's list of places to eat, let alone see and be seen. The shabby dive was a Mecca for lonely—and not so lonely—truckers, cowboys and vagrants and the women who loved them. Or at the very least, liked to dance with them.

"Look at that one over there," Tex crowed, nodding at a beautiful woman in a short skirt. "She wants me."

"In your dreams, Tex. She's lookin' at me," Fuzzy joshed.

"I think she wants the kid." A mischievous grin tugged at the corners of Montana's mouth.

Sydney's heart leapt into her throat.

"You don't say," Fuzzy mused.

All heads swiveled, and, grinning like idiots, they waved and "woo-hoo'd" at the poor girl, pointing out Syd and suggesting that she come get acquainted with the Circle BO's newest addition. Mortified, Sydney waved once, for good measure, and hoped that would suffice as an act of solidarity in this brotherhood of testosterone. Luckily, the woman had come with her own group and had no interest in the rowdies from the Circle BO.

That was a relief, but still, sitting in such close proximity with her new boss had Sydney fearing scrutiny and she dared not look left or right. Instead, she feigned starvation and buried her nose in the menu. It seemed that no matter how she restricted her posture, some part of her body touched Montana's. He didn't seem to notice that they were pinned together from thigh to shoulder, as they were all crammed like sardines.

But Sydney noticed.

The contact points were electric.

An uncontrollable wave of heat suffused her cheeks. His body was rock solid. Hers was not. Surely he could feel the difference if she could.

Never mind. There was nothing she could do about it now. She would simply have to grit it out until she could get home and disappear into her room.

When the poor waitress arrived, she good-naturedly took their orders—and harassment—and disappeared. Moments later, she reappeared with several pitchers of beer and some "loaves" of onion rings.

Sydney wrinkled her nose. She longed for a salad with raspberry vinaigrette dressing, a few bread sticks, an espresso and an evening with PBS. She was exhausted from the mental gymnastics of her first day on the job, and this unintelligible screaming match that passed for music was doing nothing to soothe her jangled nerves.

Montana poured a glass of beer and sent it sloshing in her direction, then poured one for himself and handed the pitcher down the line. "Hey, you guys!" He had to shout in order to be heard above the din. "What say we play some hoops in the basketball cage while we wait for the ribs to arrive?"

Ah. So that's why they'd suggested that she wear tennis shoes.

"There are eight of us. Four on each team. Shirts against the skins."

"Yee-haw!" The enthusiastic cry drew the grins of patrons not completely deafened by the music. The woofing faction grabbed their beers and stampeded out of the booth and toward the cage in the back.

"Come on, kid," Montana shouted, stripping off his T-shirt as he went. "You're on my team."

Caught in the tidal wave, Sydney scrambled out of the booth, panic making her palms sweat. She couldn't be on the skins team! No way. But how did one tell one's brand-new boss that she didn't want to play with him? She rushed after Montana, her head whirling.

Once inside the cage, Willie, Colt and Kenny ripped off their T-shirts and, giddy with the sheer joy of this male bonding experience, shouted insults at the opposing team and high-fived each other.

"We get the hotshot kid," Montana shouted and ran a light hand over his rippling abdominal muscles. "Skins get the kid."

"No way," Tex said. "You already have four on your team. Besides, I'm stuck with these two old codgers." He pointed loosely at Fuzzy and Red. Fuzzy and Red feigned wounded feelings.

A wave of relief washed over Sydney so profound, she nearly wept. "Yes! I'll play for their team. I'll be a shirt."

Montana took a sip of his beer. "The kid is my bunk mate. I say he's on my team." Expression belligerent, he balanced the ball on his narrow hip.

Sydney was having a hard time breathing, whether from fear or the view she couldn't be sure. He was a specimen and a half. In her peripheral vision, she could see the appreciative glances of the rest of the female patronage.

"Forget it, brother," Tex said, and knocked the ball out from under Montana's arm. "You have four on your team." He rushed after the ball, shot and scored. "We get Syd the Kid." Again Tex snagged the ball as it swished through the net. He whipped it behind his back and suddenly Sydney found herself in possession.

Caught by surprise, and still holding their beer mugs, the skins were unprepared for defense as Sydney, wanting nothing more than to get rid of the ball, closed her eyes and flung it over her shoulder. Much to her amazement, she scored. Tex, Fuzzy and Red roared victory, high-fiving and slapping Syd on the back, and the game was on.

The going was fast and furious and it seemed to Sydney that Montana went out of his way to block her shots and push her around. Figuring it must be some kind of rite of passage, she decided to ignore him. But Montana would not be ignored. At one point, they scrambled for the ball and Montana shoved her so hard she nearly lost her footing. Tired of being picked on, Sydney shoved back and knocked the ball out of his hands and straight to Tex, who scored.

Delighted at her dumb luck, Sydney laughed out loud, then remembering, lowered her voice and guffawed.

Montana glanced at her with grudging admiration.

As she took a moment to catch her breath and watch him interact with his men, Sydney could see why they liked and respected Montana so well. He had an easygoing nature and a wonderful sense of humor. It was clear that he was the kind of person with whom one earned respect.

Clearly, she had not done that yet.

And Sydney had the funniest feeling that would be the toughest job she would have, for however long she would be employed.

Earlier that evening, on the way over to the truck stop, she'd discovered that Montana was single and had never been married, due to some unspoken—and clearly unfortunate—obstacle with the mysterious Delle. She had to wonder why someone so good-looking and with so much charisma hadn't settled down with some lucky woman, in spite of a broken engagement.

But of course, that wasn't a question an eighteen-year-old boy would ask.

After the first half hour of adrenaline-pumping, sweat-producing, male lunacy, Sydney began to lose interest in the game. It seemed interminable. Hot and dragging, Sydney wanted nothing more than a leisurely bath with some aroma-therapy bath beads. But without a bathroom door, that little fantasy was moot.

The skins team was up by only two points when the waitress came and rattled the cage walls. "Hey, you beefcakes. Soup's on."

Sydney heaved a grateful sigh of relief.

"Thanks, babe. We'll be there in a second," Tex called. Dribbling the ball backward, he shoved Sydney into Montana.

Sydney stumbled and Montana caught her and set her back on her feet. She looked gratefully up at him, then remembering her machismo, roughly shook off his hands. "I'm fine," she mumbled. "Thanks."

"No problem." Montana snagged his shirt from the pile on the floor and stretched it on over his head. "Come on, guys. Let's eat. We can finish up afterward."

Reluctantly, Tex shot his last shot, and the skins were up by four at the half.

We have to play again? Sydney closed her eyes so that no one could see her disappointment. *On a stomach full of greasy ribs and beer?* She opened her eyes and stared at them as they filed out of the cage. These guys were animals.

Chapter Four

Good old Syd wasn't quite the party animal she claimed to be, Montana noted with a wry smile as he pulled onto the gravel road that led to their bunkhouse. Slumped against the passenger door, she was sleeping like a baby. He had a feeling that she was tuckered out from having to act like a wild man all night without the proper conditioning. One too many hours in the old basketball cage, he surmised. That and trying to appear as if she could drink beer like one of the guys.

Ah, well. She'd toughen up.

She'd have to if she was going to survive long enough to get fired.

After midnight he'd finally taken pity on her and, deciding to call it a night himself, offered her a lift back to the ranch. He told himself he was simply giving her a ride because they were in the same bunkhouse and all. But he knew he was feeling sorry for the plucky little waif in the ten-gallon hat who could barely keep her eyes open. There was something about Syd that was starting to get under his skin, and that disgusted him. She was a liar, and he hated liars.

Even so, anyone who'd go to this much trouble just to get a job had to be pretty desperate for some reason. Didn't make it right. But still…he couldn't help but wonder what her story was.

Montana glanced over at her, her face pressed against the window, her Stetson askew, and grinned in spite of himself. Man, she was cute. Nuts, but cute. Even without the amazing hair or a speck of makeup, she was sexy as all get-out.

Since the party was in her honor and everyone had insisted she stay, she was at their mercy when it came to getting a ride home. And though it was a weeknight, the guys had been in the mood to play darts and basketball and hit on women into the wee hours.

Being the boss put Montana in a social position of slightly more responsibility. In order to give his job a hundred percent, he couldn't stay out all night, the way the others did. Plus, given the liability factor of Syd running around like a loose cannon, he knew he wouldn't sleep a wink till she got home anyway. Her glassy-eyed stare was as good an excuse as any to get out of there and get some sleep.

He pulled to a stop in front of their place. Amazingly enough, when he cut the engine and set the brake, the ensuing silence did not waken Syd.

Diffused light from a mercury vapor lamp filtered in through the window, casting a milky glow over her slumbering form. Her rosy lips were slack and her breath came in delicate little puffs. Thick lashes cast long shadows over her porcelain cheeks. She looked so sweet and innocent in repose, and nothing at all like a male. And certainly nothing like the conniving con artist he knew her to be.

"Syd." Montana poked her in the arm. Criminy. She might be in good shape, but she was no cowboy. Soon enough, the guys were going to catch on. "Come on, Syd. Time to pack it in. Let's go, buddy boy." He grinned at the irony of his words.

Syd only mumbled something incoherent in her sleep and shifted against the window.

"Come on, kid. Up and at 'em. Let's go." Montana shook her, gently at first, then more firmly. When she didn't rouse, he tapped on the windshield with his knuckles. "Syd! Get a move on!"

Still, Syd slept on.

Montana snorted and rolled his eyes. Obviously she wasn't a regular beer drinker. Well, he couldn't let her sleep out here all night. He got out of the truck, slammed his door shut and was disgusted to note that the noise still didn't penetrate her pretty little head. After rounding the front of his truck, he opened the passenger door and Syd slid into his arms.

Yep. She was a woman, all right.

"Come on, sleeping beauty. Let's go," he muttered, hefting her high against his chest. He kicked her door shut and hoped like hell one of the guys wouldn't choose that precise moment to come home.

Sydney woke with a start.

Disoriented, she bolted upright, then thought better of it and gently lay back down. Her heart pounded simultaneously in her chest and brain. Her stomach roiled with panic and with nausea from last night's cowboy triathlon. The twilight of dawn was just beginning to creep through the windows and into her room. Morning?

It...was...*morning?* Opening one eye, she could see pictures of the Brubaker boys on her nightstand. And she was home?

How on earth had she gotten from the truck and into bed?

In the next room she could hear Montana's clear baritone mangling a perfectly nice country tune as he thrashed and thumped around inside the fiberglass shower enclosure. Her bedroom door was propped ajar and she could see billows of steam unfurling into the hallway.

"Ohhhh," she groaned into her blanket. Ahh. Right. No bathroom door.

Slowly and with great trepidation, she allowed her gaze to rove around in the dim light of her new room. Bullwinkle eyed her disapprovingly from above. She grimaced and let her eyes slide closed again. Hey. It hadn't been her idea to drink beer last night. She detested beer. Besides, she was a total lightweight.

She was never at her mental best after even a single glass of alcohol. Had she said or done anything to give herself away?

Vague visions of the previous evening began to invade her consciousness. Visions of herself pushing, shoving, running, shouting, eating, catcalling and simply trying to keep up with the guys. She moaned, mortified at how low she'd stooped to simply pay the bills.

Thankfully, Montana had offered her a ride home at some ungodly hour. She'd been slumped in the booth with her eyes closed for a while—that much she remembered. Then she recalled following him through the milling throng to his truck, and after that...nothing.

She must have fallen asleep before he pulled out of the parking lot. No doubt. An exhausting first day on the job posing as a man, and then several rousing games of basketball on a full stomach...well, it was no small wonder that the ride home had put her to sleep. After a day like that, it was a wonder she hadn't slipped into a coma.

But if she'd been so deeply asleep, how had she gotten from the truck—to bed? She lifted the covers and peeked underneath. She was still fully dressed, except for her tennis shoes.

Montana must have tossed her in here. She shivered at the thought. Falling asleep like that had been a bad move. She could only hope that he'd been too tired to notice that she wasn't a boy.

"Hey, boy!" The water shut off and the shower door slammed open.

Okay. She was still a boy. So far, so good.

"Yeah?" Her voice sounded feeble, so she sat up, cleared her throat and tried again. "Yeah?"

"I forgot to get a towel and I'm drippin' wet. Get up and get me one, will ya? They're in the closet just outside the bathroom."

"Uh, sure."

Sydney scampered out of bed and to the small linen closet he'd indicated. The shower was just inside the entrance to the bathroom. From where she stood, fumbling for a fresh towel, Sydney could see that the shower door was wide open and behind the opaque, mottled glass, there was a person. A naked person. Mottled naked, but naked nevertheless.

"Any day now." Montana thrust his dripping head out of the shower and sighed.

"Coming," Sydney said and, backing into the bathroom, held the towel out behind her back.

Montana snatched the towel. "Put a bath mat down, too, will ya? There's one in the closet."

From her peripheral vision, Sydney could see Montana vigorously drying his hair. "Comin' up." Face flaming, she rushed back to the closet and, finding the bath mat, tossed it at his feet. "There you go."

"Wait. Could you hand me the shower cleaner? It's under the sink." Montana chuckled. "It's been a while since we've cleaned up in here."

"I...uh..." Scrunching her eyes tightly shut, Sydney inched into the bathroom, keeping her backside toward the shower. Relief flooded her as she reached the sink. Down on her knees, she searched the cabinet, to no avail. "What's it look like?"

The towel came flying out of the shower and landed with a damp thud in the sink. "Green bottle."

Sydney winced and tried to focus on the task at hand. As far as she knew, he had nothing on. Unless he was wearing the bath mat. "Not here." *Please, let this hideous torture end,* she silently pleaded.

"Must be in the linen closet. Look there. But hey, on your way by, hand me my toothbrush, will ya?"

"Uh...okay. Sure." Doggone it. Was the man completely helpless? What had he done before she moved in? "This red one?"

"Yup."

She backed toward him, pretending fascination with something on the floor, and held the toothbrush out behind her.

"Thanks. Oh. And the toothpaste."

Sydney ground her teeth.

"In the medicine cabinet."

She moved back to the sink, grabbed the toothpaste and this time feigned interest in the ceiling as she backed by.

"Great."

"Anything else?" she asked, her jaw clenched.

"Nah. That oughta do it. Thanks. Just check the linen

closet for the shower cleaner. You can use it before you get in.''

She had to clean the shower? "Okay."

"I'll be out of here in a minute, and then the bathroom is all yours."

Syd searched the linen cabinet, found the cleaner, grabbed a fresh towel for herself and scrambled back into her room. She closed the door behind her and leaned against it for a moment to collect her wits. As nicely as he was built, she had no desire to watch her boss stroll through the house au naturel. With a weary sigh, she crossed to her bed and sank to its edge. Chin in her hands, she tried to figure out how in heaven's name she could accomplish her morning bathroom ritual and still remain undetected.

This had all seemed like such a good idea from the safety of her kitchen the other day. She hadn't counted on having to keep track of so many details. Ohhh. Already she was tired, and the day hadn't even started yet.

Her door burst open seconds later and Montana stood there, magnificent in his lack of inhibition, wearing nothing but a smirk and a towel knotted at his narrow hips.

"Bathroom's all yours, kid. Better get a move on, if you're going to be on time for work."

"Thanks. Oh, and thanks for…getting me home last night. I must have fallen asleep."

"You did. Anyone ever tell you that you snore like a freight train, son?"

"No." A red-hot flush crawled up her neck and stained her cheeks. She did *not* snore. Surely one of her college roommates would have mentioned that particular fact, and no one ever had.

Montana laughed. "I'll put the coffee on. You look like you could stand a cup. Or four." Still laughing, he pushed off from the door frame and ambled down the hall.

Sydney glared at his retreating form.

Using this opportunity, she grabbed a pile of fresh clothes, rushed into the bathroom, accomplished her pre-shower business as quickly as possible. Now that she was just one of the guys, there was a whole heck of a lot less to accomplish. She brushed her teeth, gargled with some painfully minty mouthwash and then, listening to make sure Montana was still in the kitchen, she stripped off her clothes and hopped into the shower.

Too late she remembered she'd left the toilet seat down. Drat.

The steam heat did wonders for her head and before long, Sydney began to feel like a human being again.

"Kid?" Montana's voice carried to her over the roar of the spray. Last night, over a wild game of darts, she'd earned the moniker "Syd the Kid," and it seemed here to stay.

"What?" Sydney poured out a dab of Montana's spicy-smelling shampoo and lathered up what was left of her hair.

"You want a cup of coffee?"

Startled by the sudden closeness of his voice, Sydney flailed about, looking for a place to hide. She jumped into the farthest recesses of the shower and lamented that her washcloth was not bigger.

"Syd?"

"Yeah?" She hunkered down under the spray, pretending to look for the soap.

"Everything all right in there?"

"Cool. Everything's cool." What was he, some kind of camp counselor?

"I'll just leave your coffee on the sink."

Just leave! Please, oh, please, don't notice the toilet seat. "Okay." As she crouched over the drain, she could see him move by with a mug. Though he was barefoot and shirtless, she was able to make out through the bubble glass that he'd put on a pair of jeans. Good. At least only one of them was naked now.

"Just holler when you get out," Montana commanded as he stepped out of the bathroom. "I'll brief you on the day's activities while you shave."

"Sounds like a plan." Sydney leaned back against the shower wall and slid the rest of the way to the floor.

That had been fun, Montana decided, still chuckling over her discomfort. Making sport of Syd could become addicting. While she showered, he grabbed himself a cup of coffee and headed into his room to make a phone call. He dialed and his brother Tex—in the cabin next door—answered on the first ring. Montana was surprised. "You're up."

"What'd you expect?"

"Thought you'd be nursing some kind of beer, or rib, or basketball hangover."

"All of the above. What do you want?"

"Well…" Montana wondered how he could phrase this without arousing suspicion. "Just curious about what you think of the new kid."

"I dunno. Syd seems okay, I guess. Average basketball player. Kind of shy around the women, but he's young. If he hangs around us long enough, he'll learn. Maybe he's shy cuz he's kind of goofy looking." Tex's yawn filled Montana's ear. "Why do you ask?"

"I have my reasons."

"And those are?"

"None of your business."

"Don't give me that raft of horse pucky. You call me first thing in the morning after bein' out all night with the guys, and you tell me you want to chat about the new kid.

I don't buy it. Something's goin' on with Syd. What gives?"

Montana took a deep breath and slowly exhaled. Might not be such a bad idea to get another take on this whole thing. "You have to promise to keep your mouth shut."

"Ohh, so there is something going on. Something about the kid. What is it? He wanted by the law?"

"Worse."

"Worse than that? The kid? That don't seem likely."

"The kid's a woman."

"Get outta here!"

"No lie."

"How do you know?" Tex was suspicious. "He tell you?"

"No. It's obvious. I don't know why the rest of you haven't noticed."

"Okay, I admit he is kind of hairless and fragile looking, but that don't make him a woman."

"Syd is a woman. Trust me. I just can't believe you don't see it."

"Yeah. Okay. I can see it. But he came so highly recommended by Big Daddy, I guess I just gave him the benefit of the doubt." Tex laughed. "So, aside from the fact that he looks about twelve years old, what tipped you off?"

"I interviewed her with Big Daddy the day before she came back as Syd. Remember me telling you about Cindy MacKenzie?"

"The hotshot woman with the fistful of ranching degrees and marksmanship certificates?" Monotone, Tex continued. "The Cindy that you and Big Daddy ranted and raved about all afternoon? The sexy, gorgeous Cindy with the wild auburn hair and the nonstop legs? The Cindy that can butcher the bacon before she brings it home to fry it up in a pan? That Cindy?"

Montana sighed. "Yeah. That Cindy."

Tex's hoot of delight buzzed into the room. "Ya know, now that I stop and think about it, that little Syd *is* pretty cute. What a little rascal. Wonder what's up with the cross-dressing?"

"That's what I want to know. And keep it down, will ya? I don't want the rest of those boneheads she has to work with to know that she's a woman."

"Why not?"

"Because I don't know what she's up to. I have a feeling she's just some kind of sexual harassment suit waiting to happen. Our dad and Big Daddy have the kind of money that attracts these weirdos. I'm just going to give her enough room to make mistakes. Then I'm going to fire her. No harm, no foul."

"Ouch."

"Well, that's what she gets for lying. Big Daddy hired her without checking her references, and I think that was probably a big mistake."

"So, what do you want me to do for you?"

"Just keep an eye on her when I'm not around. Give me a report now and then about anything suspicious you might notice."

"And I can't tell the guys."

"No."

"Shoot."

Sydney was at the kitchen table having a bowl of cereal when Montana finally emerged from his room.

"Sorry I took so long in there. Had some business to do on the phone."

"No problem." She was glad for the privacy his absence had afforded. After work today, she'd rehang that heavy wooden bathroom door, even if it took her all night.

Sydney stole a quick glance in his direction. He wore a black T-shirt stretched across his powerful chest and biceps, and his jeans were faded and snug. Neither new nor old, his boots looked perfectly broken in and added inches to his already imposing stature. Still just a tad damp from the shower, his hair curled appealingly at his nape and just over his brow. Under other circumstances, Montana Brubaker would be her dream man. A fantasy come true.

However, all things considered, a dream man was the last thing she needed.

"I was going to brief you while you shaved," Montana said, taking his own bowl out of the cupboard and loading it with cereal, "but it looks like you've done that."

Sydney frowned. It did? Her fingers strayed to the peachy softness of her jaw. Absurdly, the masculine insinuation wounded her pride. Even though it made no sense, she longed for Montana to know that she was a woman. To find her attractive.

Ridiculous.

She gave her head one sharp shake. Her ranch was at stake here. Time to get real. Who cared what this sexist cowboy thought.

"So, since we have a little time now, I guess I can just tell you what you need to know over breakfast."

"Sure."

Montana cocked his hip against the counter and, crossing his legs at the ankles, proceeded to eat standing up. "Today we've got to install the new and improved cattle-handling system. It's gonna be a big job, but worth it in the long run. Dual sweep gates, a Y sort alley, adjustable palpation cage, twelve-gauge steel sheeting…it'll be great," he mumbled around a mouthful of food.

Sydney nodded. "Sounds good." Something like that would have made life a lot easier, even on her small spread.

Learning about the workings and installation of a new type of cattle chute would be a good thing.

"We designed and built it ourselves, here at the ranch, so we know it's the best. Works like this." He grabbed several more spoons out of the drawer and, setting his bowl on the counter, gave her a quick demonstration. "The center stanchion opens twenty-eight inches. Cattle can easily move through here, see, and the horizontal squeeze pipes can be swung out of the way, like this. Fuzzy designed the chute with one-man control levers, removable kick panels, a lock-open tailgate and quick-release mechanisms."

Impressed, Sydney stood and moved to better see the silverware. "Bet you have a lot less injury. Choking, broken horns, that kind of stuff, with these." She gestured to the squeeze pipes.

Montana's head snapped up, and he stared at her. "Yes. That's exactly right." For a long moment his focus zeroed in on her, roving, perusing, studying. Finally, unable to stand being under the microscope another second, Sydney took a step toward the table and began to clear her dishes.

"Uh, Montana, you mind if I use the phone? I won't be but a minute." She wanted to call Poppy and find out if the people who'd rented her stalls had arrived with their horses.

Montana picked up a spoon and resumed eating. "Suit yourself."

Sydney could feel him continue to watch her as she headed to her room to look for an extension. There was none to be found. She poked her head out her door to find Montana grinning, his cheeks bulging with cereal.

"Don't I have a phone?"

"Nope." Montana shook his head. "One of the reasons I took Dakota's old room. Foreman gets the bedroom phone."

"Oh."

"You can use the one in the living room." With his spoon, he gestured to a phone on the coffee table, not five feet away.

It was not wireless. "Oh. Uh…thanks." Stymied, she vacillated, trying to figure out what to do. It would look weird not to make a call now. And she certainly couldn't slip into his room and use his phone.

Reluctantly, she moved to the couch and picked up the phone. *Nonchalant,* she told herself as she dialed. *Act nonchalant.*

"Hello, Poppy?" She had to keep her voice deliberately boyish, knowing that Montana was no doubt listening.

"Who's this?"

"It's me, Poppy. Syd."

"Syd who?"

Sydney darted a glance at Montana, then guffawed boisterously. "It's Syd Mac, Poppy." Before Poppy could rattle her any further, she barreled ahead. "I'm calling to find out if you heard from those people who were supposed to call."

Without looking, she could feel Montana moving silently about in the kitchen, absorbing her every word.

"Oh, for pity's sake!" Poppy's raspy laughter crackled across the line. "That you, Sydney?" More laughter. "You threw me there for a minute. So. Howz it goin'?"

"I take it they haven't called?"

"Nah. I spoke to the gal on the phone. Said she's havin' trouble with her horse trailer. Says she hopes to have her hubby bring 'em over sometime this week. So, how do you like your new job? You pullin' the wool over their eyes?"

She darted a quick look over her shoulder. Yep. Though he tried to pretend otherwise, Montana was listening.

"Oh. Well, then I guess I'll have to call you later this week."

"That'll be fine. But don't go. I wanna hear all about the job and—"

"Sounds good. I'll call during the evening."

"Ohhhh. I get it. You can't talk. Someone there listenin' to you?"

"That's right."

"Okay, roger that." Poppy chortled, loving the subterfuge. "Then I'll talk to you later this week. Oh, and if I need you, can I reach you through the main number to the Circle BO if I ask for Syd Mac?"

"That's correct."

"Before you go, just tell me this. You chewed any tobacco yet?"

"Haven't had that pleasure."

"You gotta do that. Makes a real man out of you." Poppy's lungs rattled as he laughed himself sick.

"We'll see. I've got to go."

"Bye, Punkin. Big old smooches from yer Poppy."

Sydney grinned. "Thanks so much."

Many endless, hot and torturous hours later, the pelting spray of the shower felt wonderful on Sydney's aching muscles. It would be a short-lived pleasure, as there was a sign tacked to the wall, reminding the shower user to make his stay brief, due to drought conditions. That was okay. Even a lightning-quick shower was better than none.

After a grueling—and productive—day spent assembling the cattle chute, Montana had finally called it quits and dismissed all the hands. But not before the sun had sunk so low beyond the horizon that it was too difficult to see anymore. Then, mumbling something about how the foreman's job was never done, he had retreated to the main offices to clear off his desk before heading home.

Sydney figured it gave her just enough time to wash off the grime and change into some clean clothes without fear of being walked in on by her bunk mate. Plus, this way, she could skip the morning shower and avoid him tomorrow, too.

She was brilliant.

It had been a slavish day, but more than ever, Sydney was convinced that working for the Circle BO was the best thing that ever could have happened to her. Not only would the wages help her pay off her debt, but the experience was invaluable. She was learning the type of hands-on, big-time ranching that no amount of college course work could have prepared her for.

When she did get her ranch up and running again, she'd have all the skills and tools she needed to keep it in the black. Again, she borrowed Montana's shampoo and massaged a dollop into her scalp, massaging it into a lather, and then letting the scalding water work its magic on her neck and shoulder blades. She made a note to buy some manly-type shampoo next time she went to town. Her floral bouquet concoction would be out of character now.

She'd worked hard today. As hard as any of the other men had. And they'd treated her like one of their own, too. She was proud of that. Montana had been especially tough on her, demanding even more of her than of the others. She attributed that to the fact that he was giving her the new-person litmus test. Seeing how she stood up under stress.

And he'd been impressed.

Though grudging, she could see the admiration glimmer in his eyes now and then.

Yep. She was going to be around for a while. A bubble

of happiness lodged in her throat, and she began to hum a cheerful ditty under the pounding spray of the shower.

Because of the noise, Sydney did not hear the phone ring. And ring.

And ring.

Thoroughly beat, Montana decided to check through the myriad messages and memos on his desk at the ranch offices in the morning instead of that evening. Arriving home, he found the phone in the living room ringing off the hook. The roar of the water and the steam that billowed from the bathroom told him that Syd was in the shower.

"Hello?"

"Syd? Don't say nothin'. I know ya can't talk. It's me. Poppy."

Montana grunted.

Taking this guttural response as a furtive request for more, Poppy continued. "Listen, honey, I know you weren't gonna call me till later in the week, but I just thought you'd want to know that those folks we talked about earlier called back, and their horse trailer needs a new axle and they ain't got the money. So they canceled. I'm sorry, honey, but the money you were counting on fell through."

This was interesting. Montana sank down to the sofa to listen. He sniffed and cleared his throat.

"Now, sweetheart, don't cry."

Sweetheart? Honey? Montana's brows beetled. *Who was this guy?*

"I'm sure you'll figure out some way or another to bring in some more money. Connin' them Brubakers into hirin' ya is a good start."

Montana's fingers tightened on the phone. So it *was*

some kind of scam. When Syd came out of the shower, he was going to ring her pretty little neck.

Poppy sighed noisily. "Okay, darlin'. I'll try to figure out some other ways to get the money rollin' in for ya. Until then, sit tight where you are."

"Okay," Montana whispered.

"I get it, honey. You can't talk. Roger that. I'll talk to you later."

The line went dead. Slowly Montana placed the handset back in its cradle. So. The time had come to fire the kid. Too bad. It was coming just a tad sooner than he'd expected. Like a cat with a mouse, he'd hoped to toy with her a bit longer. To make her life as a ranch hand so hellish that she'd run screaming.

But would she?

She was amazing. After her stellar performance today Montana was convinced that if any woman could serve as an excellent ranch hand, Syd could. She kept up with the guys better than he'd ever dreamed possible, understood his every command without having to be told what to do twice, and seemed almost able to read his mind when he needed a tool. Several times she'd had suggestions that had saved both time and money.

Too bad she turned out to be a conniving little witch.

Filling his lungs with air, Montana held his breath for a moment, then slowly exhaled. Damn. This was the part of the job he detested. Firing people. Even people who deserved it.

He could hear her humming in the shower. What an idiot. No cowboy worth his spurs hummed show tunes in a squeaky falsetto.

Montana pushed off the sofa cushion and stood. Quietly he moved down the hallway to the linen closet and pulled out a large bath sheet. From where he stood, he could see the shadow of her curvy form behind the steamy, mottled glass.

With a ka-thunk, Syd smacked the faucet's handle and the water stopped. In the ensuing silence, he could hear her breathing and the drip, drip of water sluicing off her skin. She wrung out her washcloth and flipped it over the bar in the shower enclosure.

Before she could exit from the confines of the shower, Montana entered the bathroom. With one swift move, he backed into the bathroom, reached around the corner and pulled the shower door open, then threw the bath sheet inside.

Syd gasped. A very feminine gasp.

"Wha...wha..." she stammered, fear making her thrash beneath the giant towel like a cornered bobcat.

Montana leaned back against the wall to wait for her to emerge. "Come on out, Cindy. Game's over."

Chapter Five

Heart hammering, fingers fumbling, Sydney grappled with the wadded towel. A blast of cool air flowed in through the open shower door, causing gooseflesh to ripple up and down her arms and legs. In her ears, there was a roaring. A buzzing. As if her brain had become a beehive. Little dots of light danced and swirled before her eyes.

He knew. He *knew*. *He knew.*

She was dead meat.

Slowly deflating beneath her, Sydney's legs felt as if they were made of bread dough that had just been punched down. As quickly as she could, given the fact that she was on the verge of fainting, she wrapped herself in the bath sheet and tucked the corner securely between her breasts. Though she was covered from her armpits to her knees, she felt exposed. Caught. Trapped.

Just outside the shower door, she could make out Montana's form. Arms crossed over his chest, he was waiting for her to emerge, but her nerves were so jangled, she couldn't move. When he thrust out his hand, she had no recourse but to take it. Summarily yanked from the safety of the shower enclosure, Sydney suddenly found herself standing before Montana and looking up into his piercing gaze. His eyes raked her over, from head to toe, and a grim smile tipped his lips.

"No doubt about it," he muttered under his breath, "the kid's a female." His hand snaked up her arm and clutched her by the bicep, pulling her up against his solid body. "And a very attractive one at that. You really shouldn't hide your attributes, Syd. Seems such a waste."

His face was mere inches from her own. If she didn't know better, she'd swear that Montana was going to wring her neck.

Or…kiss her.

Or both. His breathing was becoming nearly as labored as her own, and there was something in his flashing eyes that had her heart threatening to thrash free from her rib cage. His gaze moved from her eyes to her mouth and stayed there. Off in the distance there was a knocking sound. Was it her knees? Montana tightened his grip on her arm when their front door opened, then slammed shut. Tex hollered for Montana.

Their noses bumped.

"Don't think you're going anywhere just because we have company." His voice was low, and his breath tickled her lips as he spoke.

"I…" she whispered, completely tongue-tied, "I…"

In the hallway behind Montana, footsteps sounded, and when Tex appeared behind them, Sydney didn't know whether to be happy or to faint from fear.

"Hey, brother." There was a sardonic quality to Tex's tone. He hung his arm on the door frame to the bathroom and took in the scene for a moment. "I see that you are getting in touch with Syd's inner woman."

"Gettin' there," Montana drawled, never taking his gaze from Syd. "What do you want?"

"Well, I was just going to give you that report on the new kid that you asked for. But it's nothing that can't wait."

"Good. Then get out."

"Aww, man. Just when the show is gettin' good."

"Go."

"I suppose I can't tell the guys about this."

"No."

"Damn." Tex sighed, then pushed off the door frame with a laugh. As he backed down the hall he shook a finger at them and called, "No fighting, boys." The front door banged shut on his departure.

"Now—" the glint in Montana's eye worried Sydney "—where were we?"

"I can explain...everything..." Sydney began, then trailed off as his gaze moved from her lips and collided with hers. His blazing eyes confirmed fears that he was angry. She pulled her lower lip between her teeth and worried it with her tongue. Her fists flexed.

Fine. So he was mad. Big deal.

He wasn't the only one.

She'd grant him the fact that it hadn't been completely fair when she applied for the job as a male. But had it been fair to discriminate against her, solely on the basis of her sex?

No.

He wasn't the only one who'd been mistreated here. A slow burn began in her belly and was fueled by the sparks in his eyes. He had some nerve, coming in here and invading her privacy this way. Just who the heck did he think he was, jerking her out of the shower, and then staring her down as if she were some naughty little kid?

"Oh, you will explain everything all right—" the muscles worked in his jaw "—now."

Tugged roughly along by the wrist like a child's pull toy on a string, Sydney suddenly found herself stumbling down the hallway to the living room and then seated on the couch. Montana took a seat on the trunk that served as a coffee table, mere inches away. He spread his legs, propped his elbows on his knees and then leaned toward her, effectively locking her into place for an interrogation.

"Okay, Cindy. What's your racket?"

Sudden fury made her brave. "First of all, my name's *not Cindy!*"

"Ah *ha!*" He slapped his thigh.

"I'm Sydney."

Brows drawn, he stared.

Disgusted, Sydney huffed and, gaze narrowed, hoped he could feel the condescension dripping from her tone. "*Syd…ney.* If you or your uncle had ever bothered to read my résumé, you'd know that."

It was his turn to look slightly abashed. But that didn't last long.

"So, Syd *Ney*—" his expression twisted sourly "—why the elaborate scam? What kind of a rip-off have you got planned?"

"Rip-off?"

"The lawyers? Waiting in the wings? The sexual harassment suit? The discrimination suit? We're rich. You're not. You want to be."

Sydney smirked. "Oh, like dragging me out of the shower isn't harassment. And, now that you mention it, a discrimination suit might just be what the doctor ordered."

He leaned forward, menacing. "I'd like to see you try."

"You don't think I can do anything, do you?" She

crossed her arms over her chest. "Stupid little woman isn't capable of anything. Well, let me tell you—"

"Oh, I think you're capable, all right. Capable of conning my uncle into giving you a job you don't deserve."

"How would you know I don't deserve the job? You weren't even going to give me a chance."

"That's our prerogative."

"To what? To discriminate against me because I'm a woman?"

"No. To discriminate against you because you're a crook!"

Sarcastically, "So *that's* why you called and told me the job was closed. Because I'm a crook?" Eyes shut, she shook her head. "What are you, clairvoyant?"

"Just a good judge of character, I guess. By the way, your Poppy buddy called while you were in the shower."

Some of Sydney's bravado flagged. Montana had talked to Poppy?

"Yeah." His lip curled in disdain. "Seems that the folks you two were counting on earlier canceled. You're going to have to find another way to get the money."

Sydney stared at him for a moment, before the meaning of his words sank in. Uh-oh. She'd lost her stable tenants.

And now she was losing her job.

Tears brimmed in her eyes, spilled over her lower lashes and splashed on her arms. She sagged against the back of the couch.

She was losing her precious little cattle company. The company that had been in her family for generations. The company that she'd promised her father, on his deathbed, that she would never let go. The property and respect and knowledge that her father, and his father before him, had sweated blood to earn.

A keening wail filled her throat, and she cupped her face in her hands and sobbed.

Montana stared.

Beyond her control, the waterworks flowed and, without a tissue, she was forced to use the hem of her towel to stem the tide. But it was useless. Flopping forward, Sydney balanced her head on her knees and cried as her heart broke in two.

Nonplussed and not knowing what else to do, Montana stood and, backing to the kitchen, began to rummage through the cupboards for a box of tissues. He glanced back at her pathetic form and wondered what on earth had just happened here. Was this simply more of the elaborate scam?

He hated it when women cried. Always turned him into a mush ball. And he couldn't afford to be a mush ball. Not now. Not when he was confronting this con artist.

Delle had cried her way out of every argument they'd ever had. Because of her tears, she'd gotten away with murder. Well, not murder, actually, but close.

Montana had little time or patience for tears these days. Savagely, he tore through the cupboards until he found a box of tissues, then strode back to the living room and thrust it under her chin.

"Thanks." She sniffed, plucked several out and began to scrub at the tears. Her head dropped back on her shoulders and she waved her tissue about and smiled a watery smile. "Sorry about that. Usually I'm not so emotional. It's just that—" she shrugged and hiccuped "—my life is over."

Skeptical, Montana dropped down next to her on the couch. Pink blotches stained her cheeks and her nose was red. Tears had spiked her lashes, and her lower lip trembled. She was a sight.

Dramatically, she fell against his side and, covering her face with her hands, cried some more.

He looked down at her and blew the air from his lungs. For pity's sake, he was a mush ball. Even as he fought it, he could feel something turning over in his heart. Softening.

There was something about Sydney. Something compelling. Something credible even in the midst of this charade. Something that forced him to stay seated and hear her out. Awkwardly, he reached out and patted her forearm. It was soft. And warm. And very, very smooth. He jerked his hand back and shoved it under his thigh.

He closed his eyes tightly for a moment. "What makes you say your life is over?"

She sat up straight and struggled for composure. "Well, not *over,* exactly. But close. I'm losing my company."

"You have a company?"

"A small one. Up near College Station. A little operation called the MacKenzie Cattle Company. Except now there are no cattle." She made a noise, but Montana couldn't decide if it was a laugh or a sob. Or a combination.

"Why no cattle?"

"I had to sell them. I needed the money to save the property."

"Why? What happened?"

Weary, Sydney exhaled long and slow and then began to speak haltingly between hiccups. "My father was a brilliant vet and cattleman. Unfortunately, he was not a businessman. My mother did the books until she passed away, and then—in his grief, I guess—my dad just seemed to lose track of the financial aspects of running the company."

Montana nodded, encouraging her to continue.

"I had no idea what was going on, because I was busy with school. Just before he died last year, I discovered that he was up to his neck in debt. I promised him that I'd do whatever I could to keep the company and the land in our family. It's a promise I intend to keep. Or die trying.''

She lifted her eyes to his and they filled with tears all over again. ''And I have done everything I can think of. I have sold the cattle, the prize bull whose bloodlines my family spent years perfecting, the horses, the antiques, the cars, even—'' she gestured to the short locks over her brow ''—my hair. But it's not enough. I've been trying to rent out my pastures and my stalls, but if what Poppy told you is true, that just fell through.''

''Who's…'' Montana cleared his throat. ''Uh, who's Poppy?''

''My neighbor. Kind of like an elderly uncle to me, now that my family's gone. He's been helping me try to figure out how to raise funds. He was even the one who found your ad in the paper and brought it to my attention At the time, it seemed like a lifeline. I knew I could do the job.'' She set her chin and eyed him defiantly. ''I still know it.''

''That may be true, but you're still fired.'' He felt like a first-class heel for telling her when she seemed so distraught and all, but Delle had jerked him around just like this and he was tired of being a chump.

''*Why?*'' Sydney shifted toward him, her passion for her mission burning in her eyes. ''Because I'm a woman?''

''No. Because you lied.''

''But you forced me into that by discriminating against me! If you will recall, I tried to get the job legitimately.''

He had to admit she had a point there.

''Other than being a woman, is there anything else I have done to warrant getting fired?''

Montana thought for a moment. ''You mean other than lying about being a woman.''

''Okay!'' She threw her hands up. ''I admit it. I lied. I'm…sorry.'' Her expression softened. ''Really, I am very sorry. It was wrong to play this trick on you and your uncle. But I had to prove to you that your archaic misconceptions about what a woman can and can't do are wrong! I was the best damn candidate for the job. Admit it.''

Thinking back to the losers he'd interviewed, he lifted and dropped his shoulders. She had another point. She was by far the best. That much was evident after only one day of working with her. She was educated, savvy, strong and dedicated. As much as he hated to admit it, she was perfect for the job.

"Please." Again the tears welled in her eyes. "Please, give me another chance. I promise, you won't regret keeping me on.''

Would Delle have gone to such lengths for a sentimental reason, such as saving her family's company? Montana didn't think so. He tore his gaze from hers and stared at the wall. He couldn't think, with her sitting there in nothing but a towel. Her smooth legs and shoulders were wreaking havoc on his ability to focus.

"Go get dressed.''

"Why? Are you throwing me out?''

"No. I'd never throw you out without feeding you first. We're going to go grab something to eat. And then I'll throw you out. Probably. We'll see.''

"Okay. Fine. Anywhere but the Jubilee truck stop.'' She stood and slipped into her room.

Montana grinned. She had chutzpah. He had to give her that. And he…well, he was a chump.

Figuring she had nothing to lose, Syd made no attempt to dress like a boy for dinner that night. She finger combed some of Montana's hair gel into her hair and arranged it into loose curls around her face. With the stub of a brow pencil she'd discovered in her toiletry kit, she darkened her

eyes and then bit her lips and pinched her cheeks to
heighten the color. She had to admit she even looked a
little chic. Maybe she'd just keep her hair this way. It was
sure easy to style. She tucked her blouse into her jeans, not
worried anymore about hiding her figure. Montana knew
the truth anyway, so why bother?

Her hands shook as she gripped the doorknob. This was
it. Somehow she had to convince him to let her keep the
job. Her heartbeat fluttered erratically beneath her breast
and she struggled for composure. Okay, so she'd made a
fool of herself in front of Montana. He was a nice man.
Surely he could forgive her.

And if he didn't, well, she would just cross that bridge
when she came to it.

When she emerged from her bedroom, he was still sitting
on the couch, where she'd left him. A look of surprise and
raw male appreciation crossed his masculine features, causing his jaw to drop in a most satisfying manner.

"You're not going out dressed like that, are you?" He
stood and stepped over to stand before her.

"Why not?"

Montana shook his head, as if he had a hard time rec-
onciling Syd the Kid with Sydney the woman. He sighed.
"Let's go."

Once on the road, Montana headed for Hidden Valley
and an out-of-the-way little drive-in, where they could get
a great burger without having to get out of his truck. The
sun had set. No one could see him with Sydney and for
now—until he got things straightened out with her—that
was for the best.

His head throbbed and his guts were in a knot. She
looked far too much like the sexy Cindy cum Sydney for

comfort. How could he live with her now? It would drive him insane for sure. He had to fire her.

But how?

He glanced over at her and could see her smile uncertainly at him. Eyes back to the swath his headlights cut, he flexed his hands on the steering wheel.

She'd played the "family" card. She wanted to keep her property in the family. No Brubaker could resist family. How could he fire her when she was trying so hard to make a go of her operation? When losing it would mean breaking a deathbed promise to her father? He rolled his eyes and gave his head a clearing shake. He couldn't allow himself to be swayed by sentiment. Sentiment that she may even have made up.

He glanced over at her and could tell she was on pins and needles, waiting for his verdict. Mind spinning along with the speed of his tires, he decided not to delay the inevitable any longer.

"You can stay," he was surprised to hear himself blurt out.

Sydney flinched as he broke the silence. "Pardon?"

He exhaled noisily. "I said, you can stay. On one condition."

"What condition?"

The hopeful note in her voice tugged at the blasted soft spot in his heart. Or his head. He couldn't be sure which.

"You can stay on as one of the guys. As Syd the Kid." He rubbed the knotted muscles at the back of his neck and wondered at his sanity. *Chump, chump, chump.*

"Why?"

"Because I don't want the rest of the hands to know you are a woman. It's for your own protection and the smooth running of my operation. My men don't need the distraction." Neither did he. "Got that?"

"Yes."

They fell silent again. Montana didn't have to look over at her to know that she was beaming with happiness. Knowing this didn't make it any easier. The last thing he needed was a conniving woman—let alone one with shapely legs that went on forever—living in such close quarters.

Then again, he and Big Daddy needed her unique set of ranching skills. And no one would understand it if he kicked her out of his place. What possible reason could he give for forcing her to move out, but keeping her on as a ranch hand? Like it or not, she had to stay.

With him.

He certainly couldn't put her in a bunkhouse with any of those party-animal ranch hands of his. He'd never get another decent night's sleep.

Montana took his eyes off the road for a second and darted a glance at Sydney's feminine features.

Although, how he was going to sleep with her in the next room was a mystery, as well. At any rate, he had to keep her. She was the best, most talented hand they'd hired in years. Big Daddy's instincts about Syd were right. And considering the amount of work they had to get done this summer, he needed her just as much as she needed him. Even so, he wasn't going to give her any special consideration, just because she was a woman. No way. She'd have to hold her own. No doubt she'd live to regret keeping this job.

She might even quit.

That would solve everyone's problem.

Except that then he'd be back to square one when it came to hiring someone.

For crying out loud. Montana shifted in his seat to relieve the tension in his back. Sometimes he hated his job.

"Thank you," she whispered.

He swallowed. "No problem." An understatement if there ever was one. "You'll earn your keep."

As he pulled into the drive-in, he had to wonder just how long it would be before the rest of the guys caught on to the fact that the Kid was really a full-grown woman.

The food was fantastic, partly because Sydney was famished after a full day of hard labor, and partly because of the company. When Montana wasn't busy trying to fire her, he was a lot of fun.

They talked nonstop through dinner, and she told him all the gory details of her financial problems. He was an attentive listener and had some pretty good ideas for drumming up extra income that she hadn't thought of yet. Then the conversation shifted, ebbing and flowing and changing from her ranch to his, to the details of her job and from there to other subjects altogether.

It was late and she was dog tired, but still, Syd wanted the evening to go on. She hadn't had a night out to simply enjoy the company of a man her own age in years.

"When did you first know I wasn't a boy?" she asked when they'd finished and were headed down the road on the way home.

"Back when we shared that cigar." He grinned.

Her mouth gaped. "You've always known? I didn't even fool you a little bit?"

"Nope."

"But you let me stay anyway?"

"Thought I'd have a little fun with you, before I fired you."

"I take it that you're not done."

"Done what?"

"Having fun with me."

They neared the long, tree-lined drive that led back to

the impressive Circle BO and, tearing his gaze from the road, he studied her with piercing eyes. "Nope."

Her cheeks went suddenly hot. "I *mean*, having fun at my expense."

"That, too."

She had no idea if he was serious or teasing, but the intimate quality of his voice sent shivers down her spine. The long driveway forked off at the stables and led to the ranch offices and the bunkhouses beyond. When they reached their place and Montana shut off the engine, Sydney felt as if she knew him a lot better.

And he wasn't the ogre he'd like her to believe he was.

In fact, he was pretty wonderful, which, under the circumstances, was not so wonderful. This was no time to get a crush on the boss. Those kinds of emotions were hard to hide. Mooning over Montana would only make keeping up her ruse that much tougher. As she opened her door and leapt to the ground, Sydney knew that even though she would be sharing a roof with this man, she was going to have to keep her distance. No more "dates," as it were.

She would simply work hard to prove herself worthy every day. And then she'd retire to her room and hide out.

Out from the shadows a voice startled them as they moved up the walkway to their porch.

"That you, Syd?" Fuzzy shouted from his porch several doors down. He shuffled down his steps and headed down the sidewalk toward them.

Sydney looked helplessly at Montana, who shoved her behind his back.

"Yeah, Fuzzy," Montana returned, "it's us. We had an errand to run."

"Oh, hey, Montana. I thought I heard ya pull in. Had to come out to shut the dogs up. Anyway, just wanted to tell the Kid that he left his gloves in my rig. I'll bring 'em with me in the morning.''

"Thanks, Fuzzy," Sydney called as she peeked out from behind Montana's back. "Good night."

"Night." Fuzzy waved, then turned around and headed back to his place.

"Get inside," Montana ordered, and hustled her up the steps and inside their bunk. When the door was closed, he turned on the light and they stood facing each other. The moment was awkward as they groped for footing in their new relationship.

"Thanks for covering for me out there."

"You're going to have to be careful."

"I know. You'll help me hang the bathroom door in the morning?"

"Yeah."

"No more having me fetch for you when you're in the shower. That's no longer part of the job description, okay?"

"Fair enough." His rakish grin had her head swimming as he continued. "And as long as we're laying down the law, I'd better not catch you flirting with me, woman."

"Oh, ha. Like I'd flirt with you."

"You're flirting with me now."

"I am not."

"Are too."

"Am not." Smiling, she reached up and placed a hand against the gentle swell of his chest. "Flirting with the boss would be stupid."

His eyes darkened imperceptibly. "Yeah. I think so. And dangerous." He took a step, pressing against her palm, coming within inches of her body. "You should go to your room. Now."

"Okay," she whispered, but made no move to leave.

He reached for her hand. Very slowly his eyes traveled to her mouth, and moments later he dipped his head and sought her lips with his own.

Chapter Six

Taken completely by surprise, Sydney reached up and clutched his shirt in her fists to keep from flowing to the floor and landing in a puddle. Her heart picked up speed and thrummed so loudly in her head, she feared she'd faint. Very briefly, and very, very softly, his lips moved over hers, in a kiss so thrilling and delightful, Sydney had no other earthly experience with which to compare it.

When it was over, Montana pulled back and looked at her long and hard before he finally spoke.

"Yes, definitely dangerous. Go to bed. And close your door behind you. And lock it." He let go of her and took a step back. "Before I come to my senses and fire you."

Dazed, she nodded and scurried to do as he bid. Just before she slipped through her door, she looked back at him, sure that she'd not get a lick of sleep that night, for wondering what had just happened between them. "Montana?"

"Yeah?" He was still standing where she'd left him, watching her.

"Uh…" She chickened out at the last moment. What was, or was not, happening between them would remain a mystery for now. She couldn't risk her job to find out the answer. Not yet, anyway. "Uh, I was…uh, just wondering…do I really snore?"

Allowing his head to fall back, he looked at the ceiling and exhaled mightily. "No."

"Oh. Thanks. Good night."

"Night."

The next few days melted swiftly away and soon several weeks had passed before Montana could believe it. Much to his amazement, he and Tex were still the only ones who knew the truth. Sydney's dual life had remained undiscovered by the guys. Oh, he'd overheard the occasional banter about the Kid's scrawny build, juvenile facial features, high tenor voice and sorry lack of body hair, but these observations were made in good-natured jest. They also spent plenty of time singing the Kid's praises. And Big Daddy couldn't have been happier with his choice.

Montana scanned the calendar on his desk. Tomorrow was Friday again, already. The last Friday of the month. He flipped through the calendar pages, checking to see if he'd miscalculated.

He hadn't.

Sydney had been working there for nearly a month, without further…incident.

But it hadn't been easy. At least, not for him.

Montana picked up a pencil and, leaning back in his seat, tapped the eraser on the edge of his desk. For weeks now, that little kiss had played over and over in his mind, making him forgetful and mistake prone at work. He knew if he was going to hang on to the last few marbles that rattled around in his head, he could never pull another stunt like that again.

But then, kissing a ranch hand had never been a problem for him till now.

On a slow exhale, Montana let his head fall back on his shoulders and he stared at the ceiling. It had been tough, but so far he'd done a pretty decent job of staying away from her. Physically speaking.

Mentally, now, that was a different story.

A lot of their "connection" had to do with their shared secret, he was sure. Knowing that she was a woman when no one else but Tex did seemed to create an intimacy that was more electric than the garden variety. He could feel it humming between them whenever they were together. It was strange how they could say so much to each other without a single word.

Not that Sydney never spoke out loud.

No. Sydney never hesitated to speak her mind. She made him think. To try out new ideas and ways of doing things. Her education was an invaluable resource and he found himself conferring more often than not with her on the everyday aspects of ranching.

When they were alone, her nutty sense of humor would come out of hiding and she'd tease him, sometimes unmercifully.

A couple days back, they'd been alone for a few minutes in the tack room. When she started sassing him and razzing him about an archaic ranching method they still used, he whispered for her to shut up, or he'd kiss her in front of the guys. Cheeks pink, she'd told him to go ahead. It was *his* reputation.

It had been very tempting to throw caution to the wind and kiss her senseless right then and there and not worry about who might walk by. But he'd taken a deep breath, and backed off. To risk losing Sydney now, just when she was getting all broken in, the way a right-hand...person should be, would be a travesty.

And so far, in his studies of her résumé—researching her references, and credentials, and ordering various other background checks—nothing had come to light that would contradict her story Still, he couldn't help but wonder when the other shoe would drop. Too much hurtful history with Delle, he guessed.

Montana tossed his pencil on the desktop calendar and stretched as he glanced at the clock. Getting on toward midnight.

Nights were the toughest, as he was achingly aware that he had a woman in his cabin. Now and then, he could hear her humming as she straightened her room or simply moved about as she dressed, or...undressed.

Surely Sydney would be in bed by now. He could hit the hay without worrying about running into her.

The cool night air was bracing as Montana closed up and locked the ranch office's main doors. From where he stood, he could see his and Sydney's place over in the shadowed grouping of bunkhouses, and was surprised to note that the lights were still on in their cabin.

What was she doing up?

To be awake this late was very unusual for Sydney. Especially as they had an unspoken agreement that they would stay out of each other's way in the evenings.

As he drew near, he could hear the strains of a late-night talk show's theme music competing with the crickets' song. He bounded up the porch stairs, and, coming into the main living area, stopped short.

Sprawled out on the couch, Sydney had fallen asleep in front of the TV.

He grabbed the screen door before it could bang shut and slowly eased it closed. He pulled off his boots, then moved to where she lay and sat down on the cushion next to her.

"Sydney?" he whispered. He leaned against her hip and nudged her arm.

She did not respond, but only thrashed about under the afghan and then, turning on her side, stretched her feet up into his lap. Surprised, he looked down at the white sweat socks that poked from beneath the covers. He gave them a gentle shake.

"Sydney, kiddo, you should probably go into your room to sleep. You'd be a lot more comfortable in there."

"Mmm-hmm," she murmured, but did not move.

A frustrated groan emanated from the back of his throat. She wasn't going to make him carry her curvy little body to bed again, was she? How much was a man supposed to be able to take?

He watched her sleep. Ah well. Maybe if he waited for a while, she'd rouse and head to her room under her own power. Since he wasn't all that tired yet, he pulled her lifeless feet into a more comfortable spot on his lap, leaned back and decided to catch the sports scores. With the remote, he changed the channel to ESPN. And though he stared at the television screen, the patter of the sportscasters faded into so much background din as his thoughts strayed to the woman curled at his side.

He reached over and softly traced the porcelain contour of her cheek with a fingertip.

"Sydney?"

She sighed, and he wondered what she was dreaming about now. Did he ever star in her dreams? She did in his.

She slept nearly as hard as she worked, he mused. And she worked hard. The things she accomplished in any given day were phenomenal, considering she was such a tiny thing. He trailed his fingers down her leg and, taking her small feet in his hands, gently rubbed her arches.

Yes, it had been a month now, and so far so good. However, eventually, somebody would catch on and it would all hit the fan. They couldn't keep this ruse up forever.

As he looked at her, he noticed the stirring of possessive feelings that he thought Delle had killed several years ago. So, he wasn't the monk he'd tried so hard to be since she'd left with Pete.

And Sydney was no cowboy.

One of these days, he was going to have to face reality. Sydney was a woman and he was a man. And every day the struggle to keep her at arm's length grew more difficult.

He would simply have to redouble his efforts, he decided. Getting cozy with Sydney was not an option as long as they were bunkmates on Big Daddy's ranch. Somehow, he'd have to figure out a way to turn off these feelings that were beginning to bloom. He'd work on that.

Tomorrow. For sure. No contact with Sydney. He could do that. No problem.

With a heavy yawn, he rearranged the afghan to better cover them both and propped his feet on the old trunk they used as a coffee table. Making himself comfortable against her warm hip, he stretched and from beneath heavy lids watched her sleep.

As the first light of dawn began to illuminate the interior of the cabin, Sydney stirred. Something very heavy was resting on her hip. Something that snored ever so lightly. Her legs were entangled in a warm cocoon, making it impossible to sit up. Propping herself up on her elbows, Sydney peered toward the other end of the couch, and found Montana sprawled across most of her lower body. He was sleeping as peacefully as a baby, his arms wrapped firmly around her legs, his head cradled between the back of the couch and her hip.

Brows knitted, she smiled. What on earth was he doing in here, asleep on the couch? Sports images flashed on the television screen, and the muted roarings of a crowd filtered from the speaker. Must have fallen asleep in front of the TV, she guessed. Like her.

None of the other hands seemed to be up yet, she noted as she glanced out the living-room window. That was good. Silent mirth welled in her throat. Wouldn't they have a field day with this? Savoring this moment of closeness with the man about whom she'd just been having the most wonderful dream, Sydney stretched languorously. She could get used to waking up like this every morning. Maybe not on the couch, exactly.

The mantel clock that sat above the rock fireplace tick-tocked pleasantly. Off in the distance a rooster crowed. It was time to get to work. But Sydney, having no real desire to move, lay there for a while longer and wondered how best to extricate herself from this delicious dilemma.

Montana stirred.

Slowly his hand traveled up her hip, and then, seeming to suddenly realize what he'd done, he sat bolt upright and stared at her through bleary eyes.

"Good morning," she whispered, and smiled.

Hair askew, clothes rumpled, he grinned. "Mornin'." He blinked around the room, as if trying to figure out how the morning had arrived so swiftly. "Musta fallen asleep."

"Me, too."

"Sorry about that."

"Don't be." She giggled. "Son, has anyone ever told you that you snore like a freight train?"

He smacked her hip. "I do not."

"Do too."

Leaning forward, he tickled her until her giggles rang out.

"Shhh," he cautioned. "I left the front door open last night." For a moment he lay still and then said, "We'd probably better get up, before someone finds us in this compromising position."

"Probably."

Their gazes met and Sydney felt paralyzed.

He fell back against the back of the couch and patted her leg. "Uh, you go ahead and uh, use the bathroom first. I'm just gonna sit here for a while and...uh...wake up."

"You're sure?"

He shot a pointed look at her. "I'm sure. Go. Now."

After a long, dusty, arduous Friday afternoon spent rounding calves and their mamas into the west section, Montana decided that they should hang it up for the day. Tired and dragging, they all rode back to the stables and dismounted. Tex was in the paddock breaking a new horse and for a while everyone stood at the fence and watched.

"He's got a nice touch." Standing between Colt and Montana, Sydney leaned toward Montana and referred to his brother. "Did he break my horse?"

"Geranium? Yep. Mine, too. Most of the ones we ride under five years old are his students. Tex can tame the most savage beast and have it following him around like a puppy within days. He's really magic with the horses. He has a way with all kinds of animals. Right now, he's working on his doctorate in animal behavior, and when he's done he wants to open a clinic here at the ranch."

"Ahh. Sounds like interesting work."

"It's right up his alley, anyway."

Arms looped over the rails, they stood side by side and

chewed on the ends of straws they'd plucked from a flake of hay that lay at their feet.

"What do you do with the horses, once they're trained?"

Montana shrugged. "Sell 'em. Keep a few to replace the aging mounts. We don't need so many horses, because we use all-terrain vehicles to herd cattle now."

"Yeah, but I don't think ATVs have nearly the versatility of a good horse."

"True. But you don't have to muck the stall out after 'em, either."

"Touché." Sydney grinned up at him, drinking in his rugged good looks. His lips were curved into that private smile they shared so frequently of late. She tore her eyes away and forced herself to watch Tex push his horse through its paces.

Even though Sydney had worked hard all day, she felt strangely invigorated. It was a beautiful evening, and because it was Friday night, Montana had allowed them to quit earlier than usual.

"Hey," Tex called, riding his green mount up to the rail where they all stood. The horse pranced and snorted, and warily eyed the group on the sidelines. "I just remembered that we promised to take Syd out the last Friday of the month and teach him how to pick up women. Well, the last Friday is here, so what do you guys say?"

Montana hooted and nudged Syd. "Now, that's an idea I can sink my teeth into."

"Will you shut up," Sydney muttered before she turned to shake her head at Tex and the gang. "Oh, thanks anyway, you guys, really, but it's been a long week. I don't think we need to go out. Why don't we just stay here and play poker?"

"Are you kidding?" Tex backed his skittish mount off the fence and gave him a soothing pat on the neck. "You want to stay home, when we could be out looking for Mrs. Syd the Kid?''

The rest of the hands hooted and agreed that finding Syd a woman would be great sport, and soon everyone was getting into the planning stages.

Everyone, that is, except Montana, who simply watched her with the most infuriating smirk on his face.

"You comin', boss?" Colt wondered.

Montana pulled off his hat and ran a hand through his hair. "I don't guess I have much choice, if I want to see to it that you yahoos pick out a good girl from a proper home for our Syd."

Sydney planted her elbow in his ribs and leaned. "Oh, now, I'd be happy just to go to a movie. Why don't we go see that new space aliens thing, down at the Bijou? I hear it's really good."

Tex snorted. "Kid, you're never gonna meet anyone hiding out at the movies. Let us take you into town and show you how to live."

"Tex—" She sent him a withering glance.

Laughing, Montana shoved off the rails and patted her on the back. "Come on, Kid. You've put in a tough week. You deserve a night on the town. Maybe going out and picking up women is the perfect answer. For both of us."

A blinding stab of jealousy suddenly seared Sydney's brain as she stared at him. He was going to pick up *women?* In front of her?

Why did that thought depress her so? After all, it wasn't as if she'd allowed any real feelings to develop toward Montana.

Later that evening, after the entire gang had had their fill of the famous half-pound burgers at Ned's Lonestar Grill in downtown Hidden Valley, they all tumbled out on the sidewalk and stood discussing what would make good entertainment for everyone, and at the same time earn Syd a few notches in his belt.

"I vote we go to the movies," Sydney suggested again.

"No." Everyone glared at her.

"I say we go bowling." Fuzzy shifted his toothpick in his mouth and squinted off down the street.

Tex snorted. "We're never gonna find a decent woman for Syd in a bowling alley."

"Why not?" Fuzzy demanded. "That's where I met EttaMae."

"Case closed." Tex pointed at the Rodeo House across from the bowling alley. "I say we go there. That place is filled with women on the prowl. Just what Syd needs."

Sydney winced and cast a covert gaze at Montana. Eyes on the ground, he lazily scratched the five-o'clock shadow at his jaw. His dimples were in full bloom and Sydney could tell by the way his shoulders bobbed that he was laughing behind his hand.

With a weary sigh, she looked across the street at the Rodeo House. The place was fairly jumping with activity. The rumbling vibrations of the bass guitar vibrated in her chest and they were more than a block away. People were already lining up outside the door, prohibited from entering by a bouncer who checked IDs. The windows were blacked out with graffiti-covered plywood, and Sydney was sure that the fire marshal would have shut the place down long ago if he hadn't feared for his life.

She longed for the Jubilee truck stop.

"I think that's a great idea," Montana agreed, "but first, I think Syd needs to make a quick stop somewhere else, to get ready for the Rodeo House."

Sydney shot him a grateful look. "Yes. Sure. What?" *Anything.*

He pointed to the tattoo parlor across the street. "Let's run in there and get him fixed up. My treat."

Sydney's jaw went slack. *Anything but that.* She stared in horror at Montana, but he was too busy leading the parade to Bruno Savage's Tattoo Parlor to notice.

Swept up in the mass exodus, Sydney suddenly found herself inside, waiting for Bruno to appear from behind the curtain that led to the back room. On the counter near the cash register there was a plaque that read, We Cater To Cowards.

The walls were covered with a veritable cornucopia of artistic choices, all numbered for her convenience.

"Hey, Syd," Montana called. "Come here. Look at the bald eagle with the American flag in its beak. It's kind of big and flashy, but nobody can say it's not patriotic."

Sydney stepped to his side and gazed at the amazing, intricate, multicolored picture. The tattoo rendering was actual size—a span of at least a foot—from wing tip to wing tip.

"I think that would look great, flying right here—" he pulled her to his side, draped an arm around her shoulders and gestured "—across your chest."

He looked back at the men, milling around and studying the assortment of drawings. "That would make a real man out of him, don't you think, guys?"

Sydney hoped the granite set of her jaw would shut him up. But it didn't. Montana clearly relished turning the tables on her, and was making her pay for conning her way into this job. No doubt she deserved this humiliation. But did he have to enjoy it quite so much?

He clutched her shoulder and rocked her back and forth. "Kid, a huge tattoo is just what you need to get rid of that sissy boy image. The bigger, the better. That way, if you work out and build up your pecs, you can strip off your shirt and really show off.''

"I'm gonna kill you," Sydney muttered under her breath.

His eyes squeezed shut and his gleeful laughter echoed off the ceiling.

The guys all agreed that the giant eagle would be great.

"Or, better yet—" Montana dragged her over to another wall "—how about this tiger? Or maybe this snake on your gut. That would scream intimidation.''

The guys—except for Tex—all crowded around. Tex had to stumble outside and howl with laughter for a while.

"How about a rosebud on my...my...you know, my backside?" Sydney asked, looking for affirmation from the guys.

"Maybe the Kid needs to think it over, before he commits to a theme," Fuzzy said.

"Exactly!" Sydney feigned disappointment. "I should probably look around some more, before I make my final decision."

Montana grinned and clapped her on the back. "Okay, son. We'll let you off the hook this time." To the guys he said, "Let's go, men. We gotta find a woman for the Kid."

Thirty horrific minutes later Sydney fled the Rodeo House, hotly pursued by Montana. Jaywalking—nay, jayrunning—she crossed the busy main street and headed for his truck. When she reached his familiar rig, she climbed into the passenger side, slammed the door and fumed. As she waited, Montana trotted around the front and, hooting with glee, pulled open his door and slid into the driver's side seat.

Sydney was not amused. "Step on it, before she figures out that we're gone."

"Yes sir, ma'am." Laughing all the while, Montana jammed the keys into the ignition and fired the engine to life.

She ducked down beneath the dash and smacked his thigh. "Stop laughing. It's not funny."

"Maybe not to you," Montana said, still laughing as he pulled into the Saturday-night traffic.

Disgruntled, Sydney propped her elbows on the seat, cupped her cheek in her hand and looked up at him through the truck's shadowed interior. "Why are we just sitting here?"

"Red light."

"So?" At the moment, Sydney couldn't have cared less about the stupid red light, so eager was she to flee the Rodeo House. Finally, after what seemed a lifetime, they were on their way once again. She could see the signal light flashing on the dash, then felt herself slide up against 1 leg as he rounded a corner. He looked down and grinned.

"As pleasant as I find this position, the coast is clear now. You can sit up."

Still cowering, Sydney rose just enough to peep out the window. Thankfully, they'd left the Rodeo House behind and were now headed out of town. Never had Sydney been so happy to be leaving a place in her life. She pushed herself into a sitting position and, after straightening her clothes, snapped her seat belt across her lap.

For a while Sydney ground her teeth in silence as she watched the last buildings and lights of town give way to an endless expanse of pastureland. The countryside was so beautiful by moonlight. Finally she dragged her eyes from the view and trained her gaze on Montana, who was still chuckling.

"What is so blasted funny?"

"I don't know. Just...you. That brilliant shade of red

you turned when the guys started pointing you out to different women. The goofy way you chew tobacco. The inept way you drink beer and play basketball.''

"Keep it up. You've nearly ruined what self-esteem I have left.''

"Face it, Sydney. You are not a man. It doesn't matter that you can't do everything a man can. You are good at what you can do. Leave it at that.''

"Oh, like it takes great talent to hit a spittoon.''

"Apparently.''

"Okay, so that needs a little work. I only had one night to practice with Poppy. Will you please tell me why you are going out of your way to torture me?''

"Torture you? You think the Rodeo House was torture? Oh, come on now, lighten up. You have to admit, that was fun.''

"*Fun?* Are you *crazy?* If we'd stayed even five more minutes, I'd be eloping with somebody named Ginger Snap right about now. That woman was ruthless.''

Montana tossed back his head and let the laughter flow. "Hey, now. She was nice enough.''

"Nice? *Nice?* She was certifiable. Your taste in women really stinks.''

"Tell me about it.''

"Ah-ha. So you agree. Maybe you should tell me about your rotten taste in women.''

"Why?''

"A peek into your dating history might help explain why you are so mean to me and women in general.''

"I'm not mean to you.''

"'I'm not mean to you,''' she mimicked. "'Hey, Kid. Why don't you ask the little number with the big mazongas over by the door to dance? She looks like just your type. Hey, lady! Yeah, you! The Kid here wants you bad!'''

"That's not exactly what I said."

"Close enough."

Montana bunched his shoulders and let them drop. "If you were a guy, that's how I'd treat you."

"I doubt that. You don't treat the rest of your men that way." Lip curled, eyes narrowed, she poked him in the arm with her forefinger and took a nanosecond to admire his granite bicep. "I think you were using me to meet women tonight."

"What are you talking about?"

"I saw all the bimbos you cozied up with, ostensibly to talk about me."

"What…were you counting?"

She crossed her arms. "No."

Was she? Why did she care how many or what kind of women he flirted with? If she were to be honest, she'd have to admit that it had been hard not to feel a little out of sorts when Montana had paid attention to some of the beautiful women at the Rodeo House. She knew she looked plain and boyish by comparison and it rankled. But not because she had any feelings for him. No.

That certainly wasn't it. It was the principle of the thing.

"The number of women you did or did not flirt with isn't the point."

He sighed. "What's the point?"

"The point is, when you pull a stunt like you did, telling Ginger that I was interested in a relationship, you are not just hurting me."

"Oh, c'mon. It was just harmless fun."

"And so that makes it okay?"

"Hey. You're the one who wanted to play ball with the big boys."

"So that's what this is all about."

Montana's head flopped back against the headrest and he

looked at her for a second before training his attention back to the road. "You've lost me again."

"You're still mad at me because I lied to get the job. It's obvious that even though I work my fingers to the bone for you every day, you're still holding a grudge because I had the audacity to believe that I could do what is typically thought to be a man's job. That's why you are being so hard on me."

"So you think being treated like a man is hard?" The muscles in his jaw jumped.

"I don't want to be treated like a man! I just want to be treated fairly."

"Listen. Right after you interviewed that very first time, I was trying to think of a way to hire you. As a *woman*. Big Daddy talked me out of it, saying that to have someone as beautiful as you living down at the bunkhouse with all those men would be dangerous. I couldn't argue with that."

Her shoulders sagged and her righteous indignation dissipated. He had wanted to hire her? She focused on his profile. "Really?" she whispered just loud enough to be heard over the hum of the engine.

His head bobbed, once.

They drove in silence for several minutes before she spoke again.

"I'm right, aren't I?" she asked softly. "What was her name?"

Montana flexed his hands in irritation on the steering wheel. "Would you speak English for once?"

"Her name. The name of the woman who pulled a number on you before. The woman who lied to you. You know, the woman that I am taking the heat for."

He was silent for so long that Sydney thought she must have ticked him off and he'd decided not to answer. The entrance to the Circle BO came into view and he turned into the driveway before he responded.

"Delle," he said at last.

"Who was Delle?"

Montana took a very deep breath and exhaled slowly.

"A liar."

"Besides that."

"She was my fiancée." More silence followed this revelation. They turned at the stables and rumbled toward the bunkhouses.

"Was?"

"Was."

"What did she lie about?"

His mouth twisted. "Her feelings for my best friend, among other things." After pulling to a stop in front of their cabin, Montana cut the engine, set the brake with a vicious yank and turned to look at her. "Pete was a ranch hand here. We shared a bunkhouse. It all went on right under my nose. Seemed everyone had guessed about him and Delle. Except me. Idiot that I am, I trusted them."

"I'm sorry."

"Yeah? Well, I'm not." Montana shrugged and, unfastening his seat belt, let it slide back into the holder with a thwack. "He can have her. They deserve each other." Without waiting for her, he pushed open his door and got out. He was on the porch before she got her own seat belt unfastened.

Sydney rushed to follow him up the steps and inside their bunkhouse, not about to let the subject drop. Not when she was finally beginning to discover who the real Montana Brubaker was.

As she entered the tiny foyer area, she opted to leave the main door open in order to let the cooler air come in. It was warm out tonight.

The room was dark, except for the light of the moon that filtered in through the living-room windows. Sydney could see Montana's dark outline as he crossed over to the table next to the couch and turned on the lamp. A soft yellow glow filled the room, giving texture and shape to the comfy furniture.

She moved past the kitchen table and opened the glass door that led to the deck. Outside, the crickets' song serenaded them through the opening. A gentle cross breeze would hopefully stir the air.

That done, she looked back at Montana and, feeling suddenly bashful, wondered what to do next. Well, she couldn't stand there all night. As she walked into the pool of light that radiated from the small lamp, he hooked his thumbs through his belt loops and, rocking back on his heels, regarded her.

"Are you mad at me?" she asked.

"Why should I be mad?"

"Because I accused you of being some kind of Bohemian ape." She smiled and tilted her head, teasing him a little. "Of crooking your finger and expecting the women to come a-runnin'."

His grin was slow. Lazy. "It works."

Sydney gave her head a rueful shake. "So much for a deep relationship, built on meaningful communication." As she took a step forward, she thought how easy he was to talk to, in spite of her accusations to the contrary. He was so easy to just be with. It seemed that she could say anything to him, and though she knew she got under his skin at times, he never made her feel as if she had to be anything but herself.

Funny how that was, considering that these days, she was anything but herself.

Trying to sound offhand, she said, "Perhaps the reason

you haven't settled down yet is because you…go with what works.''

They stood for a moment, in silent tableau. She could feel the heat crawling into her cheeks as his gaze traveled over her face.

"No. The reason I haven't settled down yet is because it seems that all the women I fall for, end up being con artists."

The air whooshed from Sydney's lungs. Was he trying to say something to her? No, no. He wasn't. That was ridiculous. He was referring to Delle. Not her. He had no feelings for her. Even so, she felt obligated to defend herself.

"Montana. I'm not Delle."

"And so you're not."

Awkwardly her hands fluttered to her throat and she fiddled with the buttons of her collar. The slight smirk that graced his lips told her that there was something deeper in his meaning, and that he knew she was too afraid to delve. Unable to stand the tension between them for another second, Sydney took a step back.

"If you don't mind, I'm just going to run and change my clothes."

As he mulled over their conversation, Montana sank down to the couch and buried his head in his hands. She'd pushed him for answers as to why he'd gone out of his way to torture her this evening. With a heartfelt sigh, he ran his fingers through his hair and laced them at the back of his neck. Telling her it was for her own good would no doubt be hard to swallow. But doggone it anyway, it was the only way he knew how, given the situation, to keep her at bay.

Behind him, doors opened and closed, and from the bathroom he could hear water running in the sink.

He owed her an apology. But how could he apologize for his behavior without revealing his motivation? When he'd told her she could keep her job, he hadn't counted on the myriad complications.

The sound of the bathroom door opening brought him to his feet. He turned to face her.

Uncertainly, she hovered outside the bathroom door, and cast a glance at the clock on the wall behind his head. He swung his head to follow her gaze. It was still relatively early, for a Friday night. The guys would no doubt be out partying at the Rodeo House for hours.

They were alone.

He brought his focus back to Sydney. Her short hair curled girlishly around her sweet face and, in a sleeveless T-shirt and running shorts that revealed her feminine curves, she was a rosy little doll. From where he stood, he could see that hours of hard work kept her tight and toned. She was a wonderful mix of sturdiness and delicacy.

The more time he spent with her, the more attracted and intrigued he became. He closed his eyes. The strain was killing him.

He knew he should go to the office and bury himself in paperwork.

She gestured loosely to the kitchen. "I thought I'd make some coffee. Decaf. Want some?"

No. "Yeah." The temptation to stay was far stronger than his will to go. He hated himself for his weakness where she was concerned.

Artlessly, she padded to the kitchen, unconscious of her effect on him. Fresh grounds went into the filter and then she filled the coffee machine with water, pushed the power button and stood back to wait.

Like steel to a magnet, Montana moved through the shadows to join her. He cocked his hip against the countertop and crossed his arms over his chest. A hot breeze swirled between the front screen door and the glass door that led to the deck. Miles away, several coyotes yapped and howled. Beside him on the counter, water began to siphon up the tube in the coffeepot and drip noisily into the filter basket and from there into the pot.

He angled his head and watched as she rummaged in the cupboard for the sugar and nondairy creamer. "So you think I'm a Bohemian ape," he said, hoping to somehow lighten the mood between them.

It worked. Her bubbly laughter rang out. "Sometimes." She paused in her task and lifted her lashes to meet his gaze. He was mesmerized. "But to be fair, not just you. All of you could use a few lessons on how to romance a woman."

He shifted against the counter to better face her, and grinned. "And you're just the man to show us how."

"Very funny." Sydney laughed. "But yes. Who better?"

"All right, then."

"All right then, what?"

"Show me how." Once again, his mouth was in gear before his brain. Montana could hear the kerplunk of the last marble in his head leaping to freedom. She had cast some kind of spell over him that he was powerless to resist.

The coffee machine perked away, filling the room with its fresh aroma. Sydney touched her tongue to her lips and looked at him, eyes wide. "Uh, show you how to what?"

"To romance a woman."

"Now?"

"Sure. Why not?" He ran a hand over his face. Yeah. Why not just jump from the old frying pan into the fire. He took her by the hand and led her back to the living area. "We'll just start the whole evening over again. Pretend we've never met. Here…'' He took a step to the stereo and pushed a button on the CD player. Within a few moments, the room was filled with a mellow country-western tune. ''That's better.''

''Mmm-hmm. Much better.''

He watched as she ran her fingers through her hair, fluffing and primping a bit.

She smiled. ''I take it we are not at the Rodeo House.''

''Nowhere near the Rodeo House.''

''Well, that's a pleasant surprise.''

''Good. What should I do next?''

''For starters, you could ask me to dance.''

''Anything special you want me to say?''

She gave her head a little shake.

''Okay, then. Would you like to dance?''

''Why, yes.'' She lifted her arms, opening herself to him. ''I think that would be lovely.''

The music's rhythm was slow, so Montana took a step forward and, circling her waist with his hands, pulled her close. Together, they began to sway, moving in a small circle in front of the couch. After a bit, she laid her head on his shoulder, and the scent of his shampoo filled his senses. ''Mmm. You smell like…me.''

She giggled. ''You call that a compliment?''

''Not good?''

''It was fine. But one thing you guys should all know is that when you approach a woman, it is all right to compliment her, as long as you don't use words like *mazongas* or *hooters*.''

He laughed. ''I don't say that stuff.''

''Well, show me.'' She leaned back a bit and looked up at him. ''Go ahead and say something flattering.''

''You have very nice mazongas. For a guy.''

The corners of her eyes crinkled and her girlish laughter tinkled up the scale. "Be serious."

"Okay. I'll start over." Afraid that once he began, he wouldn't be able to stop, Montana swallowed. He adjusted his hold around her waist and, looking into her eyes, thought how a man could get lost in there. "You have the most beautiful eyes I have ever seen."

"A little familiar, considering we've never met, but nice. Continue."

"And I like these little freckles—" he let go of her waist to touch the bridge of her nose "—here."

Her face took on an expression of confusion. "Oh...I...thank you."

"How am I doin'?"

"Fine. Just...fine."

"Good. You'll tell me if I use the word *hooters,* or *mazongas?*"

"I'll let you know."

His finger trailed to her lips. "You have beautiful lips. They're perfect."

"No. Not perfect."

"Shhh." He leaned his forehead against hers. "I'll be the judge of that."

Chapter Seven

Angling his head, Montana let his mouth seek hers, and after a heartbeat that had him wondering if he'd miscalculated their signals, he knew he'd worried needlessly. Sydney stepped more firmly into his embrace and looped her arms over his shoulders to thread her fingers through the hair at his nape. Quickly their kiss flared from a simple compliment to something else altogether.

Their breathing quickened in unison, lungs laboring, mouths moving, hands gripping. Greedily they moved, satisfying the curiosity that had burned between them since the day they met. Montana let his hands slide down the curve of her waist to rest at the gentle swell of her hips.

Kissing her like this gave way to the unwanted realization that Sydney had broken through the barriers he'd so meticulously erected. Somehow, he found himself beginning to feel alive again. To want a real relationship again. To trust again.

And it scared him as much as it excited him.

"What on earth," he muttered against her mouth, "am I going to do with you now?"

"Kiss me some more?"

He did.

A moment later, he cupped her face in his hands and looked into her amazing green eyes. "And then what?" he whispered.

Not knowing the answer, either for now or for the future, made his question almost rhetorical. Their noses still touched and he could feel her sweet, minty breath coming in labored puffs that tickled his lips.

"I don't know." She tugged at the back of his neck, bringing his mouth back to hers, and again he was lost in the incredible sweetness he found there.

Behind them, someone loudly cleared his throat.

They both jumped guiltily at the sound.

"Well, one thing is for certain," Tex drawled through the screen door. "It's a lucky thing that I decided to come home first. From outside you can see in here plain as day. And unless you know the whole story, it looks pretty damn weird."

"When are the rest of 'em coming home?" Montana asked, not bothering to hide his irritation at being interrupted.

"They're a few minutes behind me. Should be swinging in here any time now. The old Rodeo House just wasn't as interesting without Syd there to find dates for." Tex leaned against the door frame, as if he had all the time in the world. "Though anyone can plainly see that we can all stop worrying about Syd's love life." He laughed and made no move to leave.

"Don't you have something better that you could be doing?"

"No. Not really. Is that coffee I smell?"

"Yes," Sydney answered, loosening her hold on Montana's neck and taking a step back. "But it's decaf. Want a cup?"

Montana stared down at her. What was she thinking? The last thing they needed at the moment was his lug of a brother settling in for a coffee klatch.

She looked up at him and shrugged. "We owe him," she whispered. "Besides, I've gotta go put some more clothes on before the guys get home."

Montana closed his eyes and sighed. Much as he hated to admit it, she was right.

"Hit me," Tex said, and tapped his cards.

Montana would like to hit him, all right. In the nose. Thanks to Tex, he had a houseful of cigar-smoking cowboys playing poker at his kitchen table into the wee hours. The only thing that made this debacle even remotely tolerable was the fact the Sydney was sitting next to him. And winning.

He shifted his cigar to the corner of his mouth and grinned. The little minx was cleaning up.

"Where'd you learn how to play poker, Kid?" Fuzzy scratched his head and sent a morose look at his dwindling pile of chips.

"I worked in Vegas as a dealer one summer a while back."

"But how could that be?" Red frowned. "You're only eighteen."

"Oh, well, I—" she darted a flustered glance at Montana "—lied about my age."

"And they believed you?" Colt hooted. "That's a riot. You must have looked all of twelve years old."

"Looked, hell. He *was* twelve years old," Kenny said.

"Well, uh…there was a security guard there named Turk. Friend of mine. Used to cover for me."

"Ah." Tex lifted a brow, his expression whimsical. "Well, that would do it, then."

"Tex, isn't it past your bedtime?" Montana wondered.

"Who, me? Nah. On Friday nights I like to stay up till dawn."

Montana closed his eyes tightly and sagged back in his chair. At this rate, he and Sydney would never have another minute alone. And he needed to talk to her. To find out what had happened back there. To find out where they stood.

It was stuffy in the cabin, even though all the doors and windows were wide open. Smoke curled in a lazy blue haze around the light fixture that hung over the kitchen table. Beer and pop bottles were stacked in curious patterns on the floor around the table. Bags of chips in various stages of demolition were scattered hither and yon. In the background, the radio was tuned to Fuzzy's favorite country and western station. He knew the lyrics to every song, and didn't hesitate to caterwaul as the conversation swirled around.

So much for a romantic evening spent dancing in the living room with Sydney in his arms.

"Earth to Montana," Tex said, and nudged his brother none too gently.

"Huh?"

"You in?"

"Nah." He took a long pull on his drink.

He couldn't concentrate on the stupid poker game. Not with Sydney sitting mere inches away. It was hell, sitting there, unable to so much as touch her. Even so, the thought made him smile. Wouldn't that perk up the poker game, him flirting with Syd in front of the guys?

He looked at the clock. For crying out loud, it was nearly two in the morning.

His mind drifted back to this new turn of events with Sydney. How on earth was he going to keep up this charade at work beneath the scrutiny of all these yahoos? It would be impossible, considering the way he felt about her.

He shot a glance at Tex, who was grinning at him with a know-it-all smirk curling his upper lip. Why, oh why, had he bothered to confide in Tex?

"Well, I guess that will do it for me, guys," Sydney said with a broad yawn, and threw down her cards. "I'm going to turn in. Thanks for letting me play." The legs of her chair scraped against the floor as she scooted back and stood.

Sydney's voice drew Montana from his woolgathering and he stared after her retreating form. "You're going to bed?"

"Don't be so hard on the Kid, boss," Fuzzy admonished. "He worked like a dog all day for ya. Besides, he's done whupped me out of my last dollar. I say good riddance."

"Night, guys," Sydney called, grinning over her shoulder as she slipped through her door.

"Night," they all called.

"Night." Montana sighed. So much for getting any sleep at all tonight. Might as well stay up and play cards.

Sydney closed the door behind her and sagged against its cool, hard surface. She stood listening for a while, hoping that they'd all take the hint and head home. They had no money left to gamble with, she'd seen to that. And they had to be tired. She sure was. But not too tired to stay up and talk to Montana.

And they had to talk.

She brought her fingers to her lips and ran them lightly

across. If she closed her eyes, she could still feel his kiss burning there.

In a matter of a few stolen moments, the nature of their entire relationship had changed. She fought the sudden urge to run out to yonder pasture and break into song. She wanted to shout her feelings for Montana from the rafters.

A small frown marred her brow.

Quivering with delight every time Montana came near couldn't be good for her hotshot cowboy image. Sydney had to wonder what would happen now that things between them had changed so dramatically. Could she still stay on as a ranch hand, feeling the way she did for him? Surely the guys would catch on. It would be so easy to see through her now that their relationship had begun to flower.

Just sitting next to him out there, unable to so much as look at him, had been murder.

She needed to discuss this with Montana.

To figure this thing out. Now.

Heart pounding with fear and excitement and longing, she pressed her ear to the door and listened. The guys were talking, but about what? Were they preparing to go?

No. They were still playing *poker*.

Irritated, she pushed off the door and, tiptoeing across the floor, flopped face first onto her bed. She still needed to brush her teeth, but she didn't dare go back out to the bathroom for fear of encouraging those boneheads—no wonder Montana liked to call them that—to stay.

Go home! Pressing her fingertips to her temples, she willed them to leave. After a moment, she lay very still and listened. The hubbub from the next room didn't seem to be dissipating.

Sydney yawned.

Well, they'd have to leave eventually. For now, she'd

just close her eyes, and rest…and relive Montana's heart-stopping kisses, until…they…all went…home.

The rooster was heralding the sun's glow on the eastern horizon when the poker game finally broke up and everyone but Tex went home.

"What the devil are you still doing here?" Montana demanded, heavy lidded and wanting nothing more than to lie down before he fell down.

"I'm so glad you asked, brother." Tex leaned back in his chair and hiked his boots up on the kitchen table. "There is a little something I've been meaning to talk to you about."

Montana groaned and cupped his aching head in his hands. "Spit it out, and then go home."

"Okay, I'll cut to the chase. You and Sydney are living here under the same roof."

"Yeah? So what's your point?"

"Just this. Considering the rather interesting turn in your relationship with the 'Kid,' do you really think it's wise to let her continue living here?"

"She's been living here all along."

"True, but if I'm not mistaken, that was before you had taken to frisking her to see if she's armed." Tex pulled his feet off the table and leaned toward his brother. "Just a friendly warning, Montana. If Big Daddy knew, he'd blow a gasket. The reason he didn't want her working here in the first place is because he didn't want a woman in the bunkhouses."

Montana dragged his hands through his hair. "I know."

"Good. We all know how Big Daddy feels about any hanky-panky before the weddin'. Dad, too."

"I know."

"To compromise that girl under Big Daddy's roof would

be the end of just about everything, including any hankering you might have to father children.''

"Yeah, yeah."

"And, not to put another hitch in your giddy-up, but you may recall that I'm next in line for the foreman job.''

"So?"

"I don't want it. Yet. I have some career aspirations that I want to develop on the side and working for you, for the time being, suits me fine.''

"I'm not planning on going anywhere."

"Well, that's good. Then you won't mind me droppin' in from time to time. To save you from yourself, of course.'' His grin lit his face. "Just think of me as your bodyguard."

Montana rolled his eyes. "Are you done yet?"

"You agree, then. Excellent. Expect me any time, day or night. It's the least I can do, to keep your butt out of a sling."

"Gee, thanks."

"No problem, brother. I know you'd do the same for me."

Before he retired to his room for some much-needed sleep, Montana nudged open Sydney's door on the off chance that she might be awake and wanting to talk.

She wasn't.

She was lying sprawled out upon the mattress, one arm flung up over her forehead, the other hanging over the edge of the bed. She hadn't bothered to undress, except for her boots, which lay at the end of the bed.

To Montana, she'd never looked more beautiful.

He longed to crawl in next to her, take her in his arms, curl his body around hers and sleep the sleep of the dead. But he didn't dare.

Tex was right. They were living under Big Daddy's roof. And under Big Daddy's rules. Even something as innocent as holding her close for a while would be frowned upon.

But not if they weren't here.

If he wanted to spend some time with Sydney, out from under the scrutiny of his nosy brother, they would have to go off campus, so to speak. As Montana stood watching Sydney sleep, an idea began to form in his head.

He and the Kid would be disappearing for the day.

But not before he had about four hours of uninterrupted sleep. After closing the door softly behind him, Montana headed for his bed.

The next day, they were in Montana's truck and more than halfway to Sydney's little ranch before either of them felt as if they could breath easy again. Sydney had to admit, as they flew down the freeway, it was exciting sneaking off together. Almost as if they were playing hooky.

When Montana had finally joined her at the breakfast table that morning only to find the broadly grinning Tex lounging on the couch and reading the paper, they'd formed an elaborate plan of escape. It had taken some creative hand signaling and winking and the occasional hurried whisper, because eluding the ever-present Tex was no simple matter. But they'd managed.

"Calling me from the bathroom on your cell phone and pretending to be Poppy that way was brilliant," Sydney praised. She rearranged her position on the plush leather upholstery of his truck's passenger seat, to better face him. "I never would have thought to do that."

"Desperation is the mother of invention. I just hope I didn't ruin the phone." He tossed a sheepish grin at her. "Never make a phone call from the shower."

Sydney blushed. So he'd been desperate to be alone with

her, too. "You might have a soggy phone, but it was worth it. I don't think Tex could hear a thing you said."

"Let's hope not." He adjusted the rearview mirror. "So far, so good."

Sydney glanced over her shoulder and through the window. "You don't really think that he'd follow us out to my place, do you?"

"Oh, I wouldn't put it past him. I have the sinking feeling we'll probably be seeing a lot of old Tex in the days to come."

"Why?"

"He's on a mission to save us from ourselves."

"He is? How come?"

"Well, let's just say that Tex has appointed himself our own little chaperone."

"Ah. So that would explain why he was hanging around this morning."

"Yup. But his motivation isn't completely selfless. He doesn't want me to get fired for hiding a girl in my cabin, because if I go, he's next in line to take over as foreman. And he's got a business venture of his own cooking, and doesn't want the responsibility of foreman yet. So I'm afraid he's going to be a bit of a pest."

"Is he going to move in with us?"

"If he does, I'll kill him." The muscles in his jaw jumped as Montana looked at her for a moment, then trained his gaze back to the road. "I guess he does have a point about us living together now, considering the nature of our relationship."

Suddenly shy, Sydney stared out the windshield as he checked his mirrors and then negotiated a lane change. "Uh, what exactly is the nature of our...relationship?"

"Well, I don't kiss the rest of the guys after a night out,

if that helps.'' The tiny lines at the corners of his eyes forked.

She laughed. "I should hope not."

"Anyway, I think Tex—and Big Daddy, if he knew— believes that I might take advantage of the situation. Coed bunkhouses were never in the plan."

"What did you tell Tex?"

"That we were big people and we could figure it out."

"What did he say?"

"That's what worried him."

"Oh." Hands to face, she felt her cheeks hot beneath her fingertips.

"I told him that we would be good when we were under Big Daddy's roof." With a playful grin, he reached out and stroked her cheek, then laced his fingers with hers. "That's why we're on a field trip today."

"I'm glad."

"Me, too. I'm looking forward to seeing your place."

"It won't be long now. We take the next exit, and I'm about fifteen minutes from there."

She could hardly wait to spend an entire day with Montana.

Alone.

As a woman. When she got home, she was changing into something—anything but jeans—and doing something with her hair. Then she was calling a little restaurant not far from her house and making dinner reservations. Plans swirled in her head.

The fact that he wanted to take her home for the day was unbelievably sweet. It was the gesture of a man she'd sorely misjudged on the day they met. But she'd make all that up to him. Feeling giddy, she pointed out the familiar landmarks as they whizzed by, and before she knew it, they were pulling into her drive.

The old yellow Victorian farmhouse sat back from the road, flanked on one side by a giant red barn, and on the other by a miniature version of the Brubaker stables. Behind the house, nearly a thousand acres of fenced pastureland unfurled toward the horizon. It was nothing compared to the Circle BO, but it was home and it was hers and Sydney loved it with all her heart.

Montana came to a stop in front of the garage and motioned for her to sit still while he got her door. It was so wonderful to be treated like a lady after so many days of being treated like one of the guys. She placed her hand in his, and he didn't let go once she was on the ground.

"This," she said, gesturing to the grand old house, "is where I grew up. It needs some TLC, but first I have to get the business up and running again. Then we can fix the peeling paint and rotten boards."

"I bet she was a beauty in her heyday."

Sydney nodded. "Mmm hmm. I have pictures. My grandfather built this house for his bride. Grandma loved the fish-scale shingles and fancy porch bric-a-brac. Said the little turret in the corner there made her feel like a princess. She bore four children and buried two on this property." Shading her forehead with her free hand, Sydney squinted off into the distance. "She and my grandfather are both buried in the family plot, down by the creek. My parents, too. There's a lot of—" her eyes misted slightly and her throat grew tight "—history here. I can't imagine losing this place."

"I can understand."

Sydney looked into his eyes and could sense that he really did. She led him up the steps, fished the key out from under the mat and opened the front door. After a cursory check, Sydney was satisfied that the house was no worse off for her absence.

She left Montana to his own devices in the shabby living room for a few minutes while she ran up to her room to change. As she shucked her clothes, she picked up her wireless phone and made early dinner reservations at Athena's, a little Greek place not too far down the road.

A short time later, Montana watched as Sydney swept down the staircase. She was dressed in a gauzy, flowery, sleeveless thing that swished around her shapely ankles and brought back powerful memories of the first time Montana had ever laid eyes on her.

She'd done something trendy to her hair, making it look all soft and chic. A pair of pearl earrings adorned her ears, and she was wearing the subtlest hint of makeup. As she moved from step to step there was a refined grace in her carriage that was unmistakable. To think that she could lasso a calf and bind its hooves faster than any ranch hand on the place was mind-boggling. She looked like the type who should be volunteering for a Ladies' Aid Society fundraiser. Not on horseback, pounding across the pasture after a renegade steer.

Slender fingers trailing on the banister, she stopped at the bottom of the stairs and he was not entirely certain that his heart was still beating.

She gestured to a framed picture that he'd forgotten he held in his hands. "I see you found my parents' wedding picture."

"Your mother was beautiful," he murmured as she came to stand at his elbow. "Like you."

"She was beautiful. And I, well, I don't—" Flustered, she cast her gaze to the floor. "I… Thank you."

As he put the photo back in its spot on the top of the old upright piano, he noticed her flushed cheeks and found her inability to take a compliment endearing. He pulled her into his arms. "What kind of rules did your daddy have about kissing under his roof?"

"Oh." Eyes shining, Sydney looked up and leaned toward him, placing her fingertips on his chest. "Well, he used to kiss my mama all the time."

"Mmm. A man after my own heart."

Montana tightened his embrace and gave her the kiss they'd both been yearning for since last evening, without fear that someone might spot them and blow their cover. As he brought his lips to hers, their heartbeats thundered like a spring storm. Together, they moved as one, in a kiss so sublimely perfect, neither was able to tell where one mouth started and the other left off.

Sydney flattened her hand on the rock-hard wall of his chest, and Montana could feel her measuring his pounding heart against her own violent pulse. For a long time, they stood in a silence that was broken only by their ragged breathing, holding each other and savoring their privacy. However brief it would be.

At last Montana broke the kiss for a moment. Their gazes clung as they studied each other in the mottled afternoon light that filtered in through the lace-covered windows. The moment was ideal. Even more so, because Tex was miles away. Once again he kissed her, marveling at the way her warm body fitted so perfectly with his. As Montana inhaled the sweet fragrance that was uniquely Sydney, he caught a movement outside the picture window and stiffened.

"Sydney," he whispered.

"Hmm?"

"What does Poppy look like?"

"Why?"

"Well, if he looks like a human porcupine, then he's coming down the driveway right now, and heading toward the house."

"Is he wearing rainbow suspenders?"

"Yep."

She sagged. "That would be Poppy. I'll introduce you."

Montana dropped his forehead against hers and groaned. "Why do I feel like Tex is going to be showing up next?" The air left his lungs in a frustrated whoosh. "This is some kind of big, cosmic joke, right?" He rubbed his nose against hers and she sighed.

"It seems that way, doesn't it?"

"Ahh, it's just as well. It's probably for the best that we get out of here, before I forget I'm a Brubaker, and uh—" he chuckled against her cheek "—attempt to sully your virtue."

"*Sully* my virtue?" She giggled.

He growled into her neck. "Kind of hard to get any good sullying done with so many people always around to keep me at bay."

"True. Although sullying me in front of the living room windows in the middle of the day is probably not what Daddy had in mind for his little girl." The unbridled laughter that Montana loved so much flowed out of Sydney.

"Probably not what my dad had in mind for you, either. Or Poppy. Or Tex. Or…Big Daddy."

She leaned back in his arms, and her eyes sparkled as she gazed up at him. "How come we get all the busybodies?"

"They're the Sully Squad."

"Ah-ha."

Foreheads together, they laughed.

"Come on," Sydney said at last, her smile broad and relaxed, "and I'll introduce you to Poppy, and then give you the cook's tour. And if we have time left at the end of the day, I might give you another chance to sully my lips."

"Don't get my hopes up." Montana took her hand and reluctantly followed her out of the room.

While Sydney heated water for the coffee and put out a plate of assorted cookies, Montana and Poppy visited at the kitchen table.

"Poppy, I hear tell you're the one who taught Sydney to chew tobacco."

"Tried." Laughter rattled the old man's congested lungs. "But she's no good at spittin'. I don't hold that against her, though, as she can do prit' near everything a man twice her size can do."

"Except smoke a cigar."

"No? Well, that don't surprise me none. Her family never was much on tobacco." He squinted at Montana. "So, when did you catch on that she wasn't a boy?"

"Never thought she was a boy."

"And you hired her anyway?"

"No. My uncle hired her."

"Ah. Must not have such good eyesight. I never really thought she made a very decent boy. Too wimpy lookin' if you ask me."

From where she stood at the sink, Sydney looked over her shoulder. "Gee, thanks."

Montana's head bobbed slowly. "Yeah, all the guys think Syd is a bit strange. Different. Kind of feminine."

"Now just a doggone minute," Sydney sputtered, whirling from the sink, empty mugs in her hands. "They like me just fine and do not think I'm feminine."

"Okay." Montana and Poppy exchanged amused glances.

"They do not!" Sydney insisted.

"Yes, they do. They just don't tell you, because they don't want to hurt your feelings."

"Well, too late. My feelings are hurt." Cheeks blazing, Sydney set the mugs none too gently on the table and marched out the back door.

"Better go talk to her. A snit just like that one is what got her into this whole mess." Poppy snagged a handful of cookies and dropped them into his shirt pocket. "I'll just mosey along and let you two visit. I'll be back later, to say my goodbyes." He shook Montana's hand and made his way out the front door.

So much for any further sullying, Montana thought. "Great. We'll see you then."

Doing his level best not to laugh, Montana followed Sydney to the back lawn. Posture rigid, she presented her back to him.

"Honey," he began softly, "I love the fact that you are too feminine to make a convincing boy. Not that you can't do everything a boy could do," he amended quickly, "except, you know, maybe write your name in the snow, but that's not all that handy here in Texas, anyway...."

He could tell by the change in her posture that she was beginning to smile. When he reached out and placed a hand on her shoulder she didn't shrug him off.

"You are the best right-hand person any foreman could ever ask for, and I'm not just saying that. All the guys agree that you're great."

Her voice was small. Childlike. "They think I'm a wimp."

"Not a wimp. No, never a wimp. Just...different."

She sniffed. "I guess it's okay to be different."

"Sure it is. And now that I see this place, I can really understand why you'd go to such lengths to grant your father's wishes. I might be tempted to put on some high heels and a skirt to save this place, myself."

Slowly she turned to face him and lifted her gaze to his. "Really?"

He cleared his throat. "No."

A moment passed, then she burst into laughter. "Thank heavens."

Sydney gave Montana the grand tour of the house. When they meandered out of doors, she pointed out all the unique touches that her grandfather had specially built or added to the house, in order to please his young bride. Hand in hand, they ambled through her mother's overgrown flower garden that she hoped to someday bring back to its original glory. From there, Sydney took him to see the barn and stables.

Hours flew past as they strolled along the tree-lined path behind the barn that led to the creek, discussing some wonderful ideas for expansion, ways to improve her land use and rotation grazing, and to set profit goals at figures comparable to other investments.

It seemed they never ran out of subjects that fascinated them both.

"Years ago, my grandfather started out with just four longhorn heifers, and gradually built and improved his herd," Sydney explained as they followed the shady path along the edge of the creek. "Since longhorn cattle were what drove the market around these parts back then, that's what the MacKenzie Cattle Company bred. They concentrated on horn and color, without compromising on disposition. Over the years, my grandfather and father bred some spectacular animals, but because Daddy didn't really understand marketing, they were never correctly promoted."

"Takes time and money to promote a quality animal."

"Daddy didn't have either. And it was too bad. Our bull would have been worth a fortune in stud fees, if he'd taken the time and spent the money. That's why I took so many marketing classes in college. I'm hoping I can learn from his mistakes.''

''You're smart.''

Eventually they reached the family cemetery. They paused, and Sydney knelt to pull some weeds away from an ornately carved grave marker.

''Marcus MacKenzie was my grandfather. He was in his early sixties when he died.''

''Ranching can be a hard life,'' Montana acknowledged.

''Well, I suppose like a bad day fishing, it will always beat a good day sitting at a desk.''

''That's for sure.''

Later in the conversation, Sydney wondered if Montana would continue ranching, once he left his foreman position with Big Daddy.

''Oh, I think so. I'll have to run one of my father's investment companies, eventually, but I'll always want to keep my fingers in the ranching pie with a small spread of my own.''

''When are you supposed to start working for your father?''

''No set time, really. We each get to run Big Daddy's ranch for a number of years, and one way or another, each of us tries to leave his mark.''

''What are your plans?''

''Improve the genetic base of the Brubaker cattle. Stress fertility, red meat yield, tenderness, taste…that kind of stuff. I'm breeding a few head right now, for my own place.''

''Sounds like you have it all figured out.''

He looked down at her, an enigmatic expression on his face as they strolled along. ''Not all.''

They'd traveled for several miles when Sydney led him across the creek to another path.

"What was your bull's name?" Montana asked as they came to a rocky area near the creek's shore.

"Roger Ramjet."

"That's a goofy name."

"Named for the cartoon character." She sang a few lines of the Roger Ramjet song and a wide grin tugged at her lips. "Daddy had a quirky sense of humor."

"Like you?"

Sydney laughed. "I guess."

There was a fallen tree that lay halfway across the water. She took off her sandals and walked out to the middle. Sitting down, she let her feet dangle. Montana took off his boots, rolled up his pant legs and joined her.

"So, Roger Ramjet, huh?" Montana eased his hat back and scratched his head. "Never heard of him."

"You'll hear of his offspring. I think the new owner shortened his name to Ramjet I. There's a picture of him on a Web site somewhere. He's a very exciting bull with some serious horn. And sweet? Would eat right out of your hands."

He smiled at her enthusiasm. "I'll watch for his calves at auction."

"Me, too. Someday, I want to buy one of his babies and start over again. But first I have to save the land. Can't build a herd in an apartment in the city."

"At least not a very big herd."

She returned his genial smile and thought, once again, how incredibly handsome he was. Yet his outer beauty paled in comparison to the man inside.

Delle was a fool.

"You know, I'd love to kiss you right now," Montana said, "but I'm afraid if I do, we'll both end up in the drink."

"Then let's head to shore," Sydney said.

* * *

The rest of the day was a wonderful haze of discussions of exciting plans for the future, pleasantries with Poppy and Greek food at Athena's. Not once did they ever address the subject of their future as a couple, but it was the subtle subtext to everything they said. The ride home was no less animated, and when they pulled up to their cabin, they were looking forward to a private evening spent on the deck, sketching out the renovations that Sydney would make on her property, once she was finally able to afford them.

The sun had set an hour ago, and all was quiet in the bunkhouse neighborhood. Montana kept Sydney's fingers twined with his as he led her through the shadows and into their main living area. When he turned on the lamp, Tex's voice startled them both.

"Well, now. It's about time you kids came home. I was startin' to get a little worried."

Chapter Eight

Montana stripped off his shirt and tossed it into the laundry hamper in his bedroom closet. He and Sydney had had a wonderful day together, and it would still be going on now, if it wasn't for the decaf-swilling busybody in the next room. Slowly Montana moved to the window near his bed, which overlooked the pond.

It was a sultry night, warm and slightly humid. The full moon's reflection shimmered on the water's smooth surface. Now and again, a catfish would jump, causing an ever-widening circle of ripples to scatter the moonlight like crystals from a fallen chandelier. The gentle night sounds of crickets and a breeze rustling through the paper-dry leaves on the trees made it perfect for a stroll with Sydney.

But that was not to be. At least, not tonight.

Nope. Not as long as Tex was out there drinking Sydney's coffee and eating Sydney's cookies. Montana had come into his room under the auspices of changing his clothes, but what he really wanted was some time to cool off. For a minute there, he'd come dangerously close to tackling Tex and punching his lights out.

But he'd restrained himself, knowing that Tex was right. Being alone with Sydney these days was not a good idea. Especially not until he got his feelings for her straightened out.

From where he stood, he could hear their light banter from the living room, and he could feel his blood pressure surge.

With a vengeance, all the old memories of Pete and Delle came flooding back. Two years ago, he'd stood just like this, and listened. Heard the murmur of voices, laughing, teasing. And with the memories came the pain. And the doubts.

Could he ever trust again? He hated himself for wondering, but walking in on Delle and Pete had left irrevocable scars on his heart.

Montana leaned on the windowsill, pressed his forehead to the cool pane and thought of Delle. Flashy clothes, luxurious hair, full figure, stunning eyes and pouty lips. She was everything he'd ever thought he wanted in a woman. A real beauty, to be sure, but on the outside only.

Sydney, on the other hand, could be just as beautiful when she wanted to, but in a different kind of way. When she wasn't pretending to be a teenage boy with a penchant for riding horses like a bat out of hell, Sydney had class. Style. Grace. He'd also seen Sydney at her worst, covered with dust and dragging after a long day out on the range.

Unlike Delle, she seemed to care nothing for the material things in life, valuing family—even if it was only a distant cousin, an elderly neighbor and a handful of memories—above all else.

Sydney was nothing like Delle.

Delle would never have worked so hard to honor her

father's wishes. She would have sold the property a long time ago and used the money for herself.

What had he ever seen in Delle?

Again he heard the lilt of Sydney's laughter, and Tex's flirtatious voice. When was that idiot brother of his going to go home? he wondered churlishly. If he didn't know any better, he'd think his brother had ulterior motives for hanging around.

Montana pushed off the window casing and dropped to the edge of his bed. One at a time, he pulled off his boots and tossed them into the closet. For an insane moment, he sat in the dark and considered going out there and accusing his brother of being after Sydney. No one was ever going to make a fool of him again. Especially over a woman.

Leaning forward, he propped his elbows on his knees and ran a hand over the back of his neck. He was really losing it. If his brother really wanted Sydney, he'd be the last to know.

That much he'd learned from Delle.

That, and how not to trust. A groan emanated from deep within his throat. These days, his mind was in such a muddle sometimes he wondered if he'd ever get it all sorted out.

The conversation in the living room seemed to be dwindling. He could still hear them talking, but now it sounded as if Sydney was bidding Tex good-night. As he listened, he could hear the sounds of Sydney going through her nightly ritual, closing the doors and windows, turning off the stereo and lights, brushing her teeth and straightening the bathroom. At one point, Tex tapped on her door to request a blanket and pillow and Sydney directed him to the linen closet. Seemed his little brother was spending the night.

Montana flopped back on his bed and contemplated the shadows on the ceiling.

Sydney woke to the sounds of strange tapping noises on her bedroom window. Blinking in confusion, she sat up in bed and ran her hands over her eyes. As she peered over at the window, and saw the shadowy outline of a man peering in, her first instinct was to scream bloody murder, and then rush to the safety of Montana's room. That is, until she realized that the prowler in question, was none other than Montana. What on earth was he doing here at this hour? It couldn't be much past midnight.

Throwing back the sheet, Sydney slipped from her bed and padded to the window. She unfastened the lock and threw up the sash.

"Are we eloping?" she teased and then covered her mouth to stifle a broad yawn.

"I can see the idea excites you." His grin was boyish and vulnerable.

"If this is a proposal, you need lessons."

His warm chuckle rumbled in her ear as he leaned in through the window and nuzzled her neck. "More lessons? Great. When do we start?"

"Montana, not that I'm not enjoying this midnight rendezvous, but I'm dying of curiosity. What are you doing here? It can't be morning, it's still dark outside. Come in, before you get eaten alive by mosquitoes."

"Mmm," he whispered, and, cupping her cheeks through the window, lightly kissed her lips. "Don't tempt me. I can't risk the unholy hullabaloo that would erupt if Officer Tex found out that I was in here with you, however innocent it might be."

She smiled against his smile. "So, if we're not eloping,

and you're not here to sully my virtue, then why are you here?''

''Pancakes.''

''Pancakes? At midnight?''

''It's not midnight.''

''Then what time is it?''

''Almost five.''

''Really?'' She reared back in surprise and then frowned. ''Five? But it's Sunday!''

''Shhh.'' He nodded toward her door. ''Tex.''

''Sorry. But it is Sunday.''

''I know, but I thought if we got out of here early enough, we could go out to breakfast and then take a drive. I have the truck all loaded up with everything we could possibly need for the whole day. This afternoon, I thought we could go to the rodeo.''

Excitement coursed through her body. She hadn't been to a rodeo in ages. Without a word, Sydney disappeared and began throwing her clothing out the window.

Montana laughed. ''I'll take it that this is a yes.'' He gathered up her clothing and toiletries bag and began stuffing them into the backpack she flung out on top of them.

''You have only to say the word *rodeo*,'' she said sotto voce, ''and I'm there. Unless—'' she paused and peered out the window at him ''—you're referring to the Rodeo House, in which case you can count me out.''

''You're in luck. The Rodeo House isn't open for breakfast.''

Sydney leaned out the window and held her arms open wide. ''Then I'm all yours.''

''And I'm…'' With a sigh, he took her around the waist and lifted her from the window and into his arms, and muttered under his breath, ''A chump.''

"Pardon?"

"Lucky. I'm a lucky guy."

Montana's truck was parked in front of their bunkhouse. As quietly as they could, they closed the cab doors and then, leaning back, exhaled hugely with relief.

"Hand me my boots," Sydney whispered.

"Sure, but why are you whispering?"

She giggled. "I don't know."

"We're safe. No one can hear us. Come here."

She slid into his embrace and when his warm mouth closed over hers, Sydney felt as if she'd finally come home. Whole, after years of being only half of something far greater than she'd ever imagined. She was falling. Deeper and deeper and...deeper.

Back in the recesses of her mind a worry niggled about how falling in love with Montana fit into future plans for her ranch. He was needed by his family, and eventually her full attention would be taken by her own property.

Melting under his touch, she pushed the distracting thoughts aside. She'd cross that bridge when they came to it. For now, she'd simply enjoy the magic they shared whenever they were together.

Montana sighed a contented sigh and framed her face in his hands. "We'd better get out of here. It's starting to get light."

"Yeah," she whispered, but made no move.

"You are turning my brain to mush."

"Me?"

"Yes, you."

"How so?"

"I don't even know. My brain is too mushy to answer that question."

She giggled. "I love your mushy brain."

"The feeling is mutual."

"Mmm." He loved her brain. Sydney decided she'd take that out and analyze that later. For now, she'd be content to relish another wonderful kiss. She allowed her head to loll back in the cradle of his arms and her eyes to drift shut. The man could kiss, she had to give him that. Of their own volition, her arms rose and circled his neck.

After a long moment, he whispered, "What's my name?"

Her laughter was low in her throat. "Some state. North of here, I believe. Oklahoma?"

He pulled back and gazed deeply into her eyes. "That must be it." A quick glance over her shoulder had him beating the steering wheel in frustration.

"What?"

"Sully squad."

Laughter burbled into her throat. "Which one?"

"Fuzzy. Quick. Get down."

Sydney scrambled off the seat and huddled down on the floorboards. Montana shook open the Sunday paper and scattered it over her head.

"Stop laughing," he ordered, obviously battling his own mirth. "You're going to get us in trouble."

"Sorry." The paper rattled as she shook. Face buried in her hands, she bit her tongue to stem the flow of hilarity. She could hear Montana buzzing his window down.

"Hey, Fuzzy, how you doing this morning?"

"Great. Just great. You're sure up awful early for a Sunday morning. Church don't start for hours."

"That's true, but I've got some other plans for today."

Fuzzy leaned on the door and settled in for some conversation. "That right? Where ya goin'?"

"Uh...thought I'd take in a rodeo."

"Gettin' a mighty early start."

"Want a good seat."

"I hear that. Rodeo, huh? Now, that sounds like a good time. You want some company?"

"Oh…well, I…you know…"

"Hupp…never mind. I just remembered. I'm meetin' EttaMae after Sunday school and we're going to a craft show."

The newspaper rattled as Sydney battled the laughter. Montana shoved her clothes and boots off the seat and onto her head. She grunted.

"Craft show, huh?"

"Yeah, all kinds of decorations and doodads made out of yarn. It's kind of dull, but there is always stuff to eat, so I go."

"Well, Fuzzy, I'm sorry you can't join me—" Montana started the engine "—but I understand. When a woman calls, you go."

Fuzzy laughed. "Yep. That's how it is, all right. Well, you enjoy the rodeo. Maybe you'll meet a nice woman there."

"That's my hope."

With a jaunty salute, Fuzzy stepped back. "Good luck."

"Thank you, Fuzzy. I have a good feeling."

Sydney's laughter rang out as Montana pulled onto the gravel road and sped off. He checked the rearview mirror and said, "If the strange look on Fuzzy's face is any indication, I think he just heard you laugh."

"Probably thought it was you." The thought made Sydney laugh harder as she crawled up onto her seat and, thrusting her feet onto the dash, struggled into her boots.

"You're weird." Grinning, Montana grabbed her ankle and shook it.

By that afternoon, they were sitting in the stands at an outdoor rodeo, about an hour outside Dallas. Sydney was so glad Montana had thought of this. The rodeo was one of her very favorite things in the whole world, and she hadn't had time to go in ages.

All the familiar sights and smells brought a flood of memories of her high school days rushing back. The musty aroma of dirt, manure and old wood mingled with those of grilled ribs and mass humanity. The milling crowd moved into their seats carrying piles of popcorn, cotton candy, hot dogs, drinks and cameras for capturing special moments. Excited children pointed out decorated cowboys and decorated horses carrying decorated rodeo princesses. One small child was heard to murmur in awe, "So this is what it's like, inside the radio."

Hooves churned up the dirt in the arena until the announcer brought everyone to their feet for the national anthem. When that was over, wild applause signaled the beginning of that day's events.

"Wonder what Tex is doing right about now?" Montana mused as they settled back to enjoy the show.

Sydney giggled. "Probably thinking up ways to booby-trap our windows."

"I have to admit, we were pretty sneaky this morning."

"That was fun." She reached into the popcorn box and fed first Montana, and then herself. "You know, someday he's not going to follow us around anymore, and I think life will be much less exciting."

"Oh..." Montana shot her a pointed look. "I wouldn't necessarily say that."

She could feel her cheeks grow warm at the implied message, but was luckily saved by the bull. As if everyone were holding their collective breath, the crowd noise dimmed, just before the chute burst open and a bull-shaped thrashing machine erupted. Hooves flung mud like missiles as the bull kicked and twisted, jerking his rider around like a one-armed rag doll.

Eight seconds passed like eighty.

Finally, the whistle signaled the end of his ride and, jaw set with a victory smirk, the cowboy jumped off the bovine tornado, ignored the screaming crowd and swaggered back toward the chutes.

He made it.

Cameras flashed, people consulted their programs and everyone breathed a sigh of relief.

"You used to do that, huh?" Sydney asked.

"Yep."

"I love the rodeo, but I could never understand what makes a man want to do that."

"It's there."

Sydney laughed. "Okay. That, I can understand. But once you've conquered it, and lived to tell the tale, why keep it up? It's so brutal."

"I was addicted to it."

"Addicted to pain?"

"No. To the rush. I think the high is so phenomenal because you know that once the chute opens, there is no going back. You cross the line and the grim reaper might just be waiting on the other side. If you can cross the line and come back, then you win."

Sydney rolled her eyes. "Must be a guy kind of thing. To me, you win if you don't cross that particular line."

"You're a woman."

"You know—" she thoughtfully chewed her popcorn "—I used to take a comment like that as an insult, but now I see it more as a badge of honor. Wisdom." She grinned. "Besides, I think—and I feel qualified to say this now— being a woman is much nicer than being a man."

"I'm sure glad you're a woman." He kissed the tip of her nose.

"So you've finally come around." She couldn't resist teasing him.

"I've seen the light."

Time seemed suspended as they smiled into each other's eyes. Moments later, their attention was brought back to the arena by the announcer's voice, and a split second after that another bull came blasting out of the chute.

Sydney winced as this cowboy was bucked off and then stepped on by the outraged bull. "Mm, mm, mmm. No pain, no pain. That's my motto."

Several clowns rushed to his side and helped him back up to his feet. The crowd cheered and the cowboy shot them a thumbs-up.

Montana twined his fingers with hers. "Hey, you ain't a cowboy if you haven't had at least one concussion," He ran his free hand over his unshaven jaw. "Bull riding is one of those events where people understand that the guy coming out of the chute might not get up again. In a very macabre way, it's exciting. Life-and-death stuff. The modern-day version of throwing the Christians to the lions."

"Oh, what fun. Why did you quit?"

"Got too old."

"Mmm. That's one of the reasons I quit barrel racing."

"But you're only eighteen, Kid."

"And some months."

As they laughed, a little boy in the seat in front of them peeked between the chair backs at them, staring and smiling. No more than three years old, he had red cheeks that were baby plump and his jet-black hair stood straight up on end.

Montana pulled his hat over his face, and then flicked it back with his thumb, playing peekaboo with the boy for a while. Delighted, the child giggled and hid behind his seat before staring through the cracks. Back and forth he went, giggling all the while as they waited for the next bull to come rocketing out of the chute.

"I think he likes you," Sydney murmured.

Montana nodded and grinned. "Of course he does. I'm a Brubaker. We're kid magnets."

"You want to have a bunch of kids?"

"I don't know. Probably. My mom and dad sure did."

"How many brothers and sisters do you have?"

"Eight."

"Eight? There are *seven* more just like Tex at home?"

"No. Some of 'em are worse than him."

She groaned.

He angled his head to better study her face. "What about you? Do you want to have a big family?"

"I think so. Maybe not nine kids, but a couple little cowboys or cowgirls might be nice."

The announcer's voice boomed over the PA system, joking with the clown.

The clown said, "Ohhh, I had a rough night last night."

The announcer took the bait. "What happened?"

"My dear wife pounded me to a bloody pulp."

"I thought your wife was up in New Jersey, visiting her mother."

"I did, too."

When the laughter had died down, everyone's attention turned to another one of the clowns, who'd donned a giant bull's head. Children laughed as smoke poured out of his nostrils. With his foot he pawed at the ground and, lowering his head, pretended to charge at the chute where another bull was being readied for a ride.

"What's your favorite event?" Montana wondered.

"To participate in, or to watch?"

"To participate in."

"Well…" She gestured down to the arena. "I love to barrel race."

"I bet you're good."

"With the right horse, I'm okay."

"What's your favorite event to watch?"

"I don't know. I guess the wild mustang race, just because it's so fun to watch those guys try to saddle an unbroken animal and then try to ride it across the finish line."

"Yeah. I did that once. I'd rather ride a bull." His eyes strayed to the chutes, where they could see the top of a cowboy's head as he mounted. "I still remember what it feels like behind the chutes. It's strangely quiet back there. Mostly because everyone is praying, I guess."

"Same thing for barrel racers and calf ropers, but probably not as intense."

The PA system crackled and it was announced that this was to be Jake Monroe's last ride, as the cowboy was retiring after today.

"Hey, you know, I think I know this guy." Montana opened his program and scanned the list of bull riders. "I do know him. Jake Monroe. You've gotta see this. This guy has been on the circuit for years. Must be at least thirty-five. He was around back when I rode."

"Wow. Old man."

Montana reached up and ruffled her hair. "For the rodeo, he's a geezer."

"I think I've heard of him."

"No doubt. Several years ago he broke his back, his knees are shredded and he's had more concussions than Big Daddy's got kids. He's been skunked by this bull—" he gestured to the chute "—Maddog more than once. According to this—" he held up his program "—today it's do or die."

Sydney covered her eyes. "I hope he lives."

The audience drew a collective breath as the bull named Maddog came blasting out of the chute, bouncing old Jake like a dog's tug toy on his back. Jake's form was perfect and the swell of applause grew as the time passed, second by agonizing second. Everything pointed to victory for old Jake, until something went seriously wrong. Before anyone could blink, Jake was lying in an unconscious heap on the ground. The rodeo clowns distracted Maddog from committing any further crime, and soon he was lassoed and brought back to his holding pen.

Wide-eyed, Sydney looked at Montana, and clutched his hand.

Over the loudspeaker the rodeo announcer said, "All you believers know what to do." The arena went silent and Jake's wife scrambled down the ladder from the stands and ran to her husband's side. An ambulance that had been waiting in the wings pulled into the arena, and the paramedics rushed to Jake. There was a moment of silence as the cowboy was carefully lifted onto a stretcher. Jake waved weakly and as they loaded him inside, the crowd stood and gave him a respectful ovation, commemorating a long, if not always successful, career.

"I'm so glad you don't do this anymore," Sydney whispered. "I couldn't stand it, if that was you down there."

Montana looped an arm around her shoulders and, tipping her chin with his forefinger, searched her face. The fear in her expression was real, and he could see that she was thinking back to his rodeo days and worrying retroactively.

"I'm not Jake," he whispered.

Sydney sighed. "And so you're not."

The ride home was relaxed, with lazy conversation after a wonderful day spent away from life's daily vicissitudes.

Sydney was slumped against the passenger door of Montana's truck as they took the back roads home. Helpless with laughter, Sydney listened to Montana regale her with wild tales of a youth spent with eight precocious siblings.

"I'm jealous," she finally said, pushing herself upright and swiping at the tears of hilarity in her eyes. "As an only child, I always wanted a little brother or sister."

"Yeah? Well, there were days I wanted to be an only child. Thought that just this morning, when I saw Tex sprawled out on the floor between our bedrooms."

"How many of you Brubakers are there altogether, anyway?"

"Well, I come from a pretty big family. It's not too hard keeping 'em all straight, if you just remember that my father's older brother is a huge fan of country music. Big Daddy Brubaker has nine kids, all named after country-western singers."

Sydney's delighted laughter made him smile. "You're kidding."

"Nope. There's Conway, Merle, Buck, Patsy, Johnny, Kenny, the twins, Waylon and Willie, and Hank."

"Wow."

"Yeah. Anyway, my dad and mom also have nine kids. I'm the second oldest after Dakota. When it came to naming us, my dad—being a real patriot—named us for states of the union. Anyhow, there are four boys—Dakota, me, Tex and Kentucky who goes by Tucker. There are five girls—Virginia, who everyone calls Ginny, then Carolina, Georgia, Maryland, who goes by Mary, and last but not least, little Louise-Anna. She's still in high school."

Sydney counted on her fingers. "Wow. That's eighteen of you right there. Are there any more?"

"Well, Big Daddy and my dad have two younger brothers. Buford named his kids after car brands—Ford, Chevy, Porsche, Dodge and Mercedes. And Harlan named his kids after months—April, May, June, July, Augustus and Jason.''

"Jason?"

"Stands for July, August, September, October and November. His mother drew the line when Uncle Harlan wanted to name him September. There are other branches of the Brubaker family tree, in other states, but I'll have to call my mom and get the skinny on everyone, if you want more details.''

"No, no. My head is swimming as it is.'' Sydney propped her elbow on the seat rest and cupped her cheek in her hand. "I only have one cousin, Ray. Retired air force. Lives in Oklahoma. I see him every few years. Other than him, Poppy is the only real family I have.''

It was still relatively early when they arrived back at the Circle BO. Sydney hid under the newspaper until they were safely parked, and then, when the coast was clear, jumped out of the passenger side door, bounded up the stairs and slipped inside their front door. Montana was right behind her.

"Tex?'' Sydney called as she peeked around the living area. They moved to their bedrooms and, poking their heads in, looked around.

"Not here,'' Montana said. "Must have gotten tired of waiting for us and gone home.''

"Dare we dream?''

Taking her by the hand, Montana tugged her back to the living room and over to the couch. Together they sank into the thickly stuffed cushions. Once they were settled, he gathered her into his arms and rested his forehead against hers.

Their kiss had only just begun when the sound of Tex's voice intruded.

"There you are!" he said, coming through the glass doors that led from the deck. He was wearing an apron with a tuxedo silk-screened on the front and holding barbecue tools in his mittened hands. "Just in time. I took the liberty of barbecuing some ribs. Invited the guys. Everyone should be here in about a half hour."

"I'm gonna kill him," Montana muttered.

Chapter Nine

"Montana, honey, I don't think beating up on your little brother is such a good idea."

Sydney stepped between the two men and placed a placating hand on each broad chest.

"Why not?" Montana ground out the words. His expression was murderous, and the thunderclouds were fairly visible above his head.

Sydney clutched the placket of Tex's shirt and, crushing the fabric, she stood on tiptoe and tugged his face down to hers. "Because *I* want to!" she shouted.

"Easy, tiger." With a grin, Montana put an arm around her waist and pulled her out of striking distance.

"Some thanks." Tex feigned wounded feelings. "I save you two from yourselves, and what do I get? Beat up for my trouble. That's cold."

Sydney studied Montana's brother levelly for a moment and then let out a long, slow breath. "Tex, dear, I'm used to living alone. I find having someone breathing down my neck and monitoring my every move a bit disconcerting.

But I can adjust to that. The thing that is driving me absolutely nuts though, is your constant need to entertain at our house.''

"Our house?'' The knowing grin and the arch in Tex's brow spoke volumes.

"Our *bunk*house,'' she amended, face flaming. "Our *cabin*.''

"Oh, I know what you meant.''

Montana rested his chin on the top of Sydney's head. "Kind of makes all those lonely days as an only child worthwhile, huh?''

"I'll say,'' Sydney groused.

"Aw, come on, you guys. This is gonna be fun. Fuzzy had EttaMae make potato salad and everything. Big Daddy said he might stop by for dessert later. You know how he loves a rousing game of horseshoes by moonlight.'' Tex winked at Sydney. "You'll love it, Syd. Very romantic.''

Montana groaned. "Just exactly how long is this shindig going to last?''

"Till everyone gets tired or the food runs out, whichever comes first. I, of course, will be crashing here.''

Wriggling in Montana's arms and wishing she could reach Tex's throat, Sydney questioned, "Tex, doesn't Kenny wonder why you're never home anymore?''

"Nah. Kenny's got a new girlfriend. He's gone a lot these days.'' Tex scratched his jaw with the edge of his spatula. "Listen up, you guys. The coals in the pit have been on for an hour. They'll be perfect pretty soon. I could really use a hand.''

Shoulders wilting, Sydney tipped her chin back and looked at Montana. "I guess we don't have much choice.''

Montana shrugged. "If you can't beat 'em…''

Montana's arms still snug at her waist, Sydney turned

and whispered up at him. "I can't, but maybe together we could get in a few good licks."

"After everyone leaves. It's a date."

Ignoring their banter, Tex gestured to the top buttons on his shirt. "Oh, and Syd, before everyone gets here, you might want to button up. You're looking a bit more feminine than usual."

Sydney stuck out her tongue. "Tex, go away."

Laughter echoed off the ceiling as Tex turned and sauntered toward the kitchen.

Montana turned her in his arms and slowly buttoned the top two buttons of her shirt. "Don't listen to him, honey. I don't think you look a bit feminine. I think you look big and mean and tough, like a sweaty old gorilla."

With a saucy grin, Sydney rested her palms at his lower back. "You're just saying that to make me feel good."

Montana laughed. "Come on. Let's go give him a hand. The sooner we get this show on the road, the sooner everyone will leave."

Seated at one of the three picnic tables behind the grouping of cabins, Montana conversed with Big Daddy while everyone else played horseshoes out on the lawn. EttaMae had tucked a four-layer chocolate cake with fudge frosting into the basket next to her potato salad. In hog heaven, Big Daddy was busy wrapping his lips around a generous slice of that, with a scoop of homemade ice cream on the side.

As delicious as it was, Montana could only toy with his own dessert. Covertly he watched Sydney play horseshoes with the guys by the light of a few blazing torches. It looked as if they were having fun. He'd have joined them, except for the fact that he might forget himself and reach for Sydney in a way that would cast suspicion on the nature of their relationship.

For the dozenth time in as many seconds, he wished that they were alone. It was already after ten o'clock, and the play showed no signs of slowing. But who could blame them? It was still as muggy and warm as noonday. Because Big Daddy had a global conscience, the air-conditioning units in each cabin did not come on until lights-out. And when they did, it was still too warm to sleep well.

Even the bugs were committing suicide in droves, diving into the purple light of the bug zapper as if to escape the heat once and for all. The constant *zzztt* was almost musical.

Sydney's throaty laughter wafted through the shadows, creating in Montana a yearning for something he hadn't wanted since he'd proposed to Delle. As that realization dawned, he clutched his fork until his hand shook. Somewhere in the recesses of his addled brain, was he considering proposing to Sydney? Could he take that chance? Could he learn to trust again?

No. Montana blew out a deep breath and rotated his shoulders. No. Not yet. He needed more time to heal. Much more time. Maybe the rest of his life.

Although it was becoming increasingly obvious that no matter how he vowed to stay away from her, she attracted him like a bug to a zapper. *Zzztt.*

Aww. He was dead meat.

Again Sydney laughed, and the sound of her voice set off an explosive reaction in his body. Deep in his chest, his heart thundered. His stomach twisted, his palms sweated, his mouth went dry and his spine felt as if it were conducting electricity. *Zzztt. Zzztt.*

It boggled his mind that no one could tell that Sydney was a woman. That sexy alto was a dead giveaway. Criminy, a blind man could tell.

"Mmm, mmm, mmm. That is some good eats." Big

Daddy pushed back his plate and belched contentedly. "That EttaMae sure can bake. I oughta offer her a job in my kitchen."

Montana slowly surfaced from his reverie and nodded. "She'd probably like seeing more of Fuzzy."

"You don't say? Well, then, it's a done deal. Gotta keep our hands happy. Speakin' of happy, how is the Kid working out for you?"

Montana squinted through the duskiness to Sydney's slender silhouette. "Fine."

"Fine? You don't sound too enthused. You know, Syd's sixty-day probation is gonna be up pretty quick. If you have any problems, we should take care of them now."

"No. I like him." More than Big Daddy would ever know.

"Well, good. I thought you would, the minute I laid eyes on that kid. I said to myself, this is the one."

"And you were right. This time." With his fork, Montana stabbed a bite of cake and then pointed it loosely at his uncle. "Although next time, it probably wouldn't hurt to spend a little more time checking references."

"Didn't need to. I got a sixth sense about this kind of stuff."

It was all Montana could do not to laugh. Some sixth sense. Big Daddy had missed the most glaringly obvious bit of information about his new hire.

"A good helpmate is hard to come by." Big Daddy wiped his pliant smile on a large linen napkin and regarded Montana over the flicker of the citronella candle that burned on the table. "You know, even though all of our men are talented hands and hard workers, I knew it would take a special personality to work alongside you, day in and day out. None of 'em seemed to have the temperament, let alone the interest, for that kind of job. We were very lucky to find this one for you.''

As they chatted, Tex bounded up the steps to the deck and inserted himself into the conversation. ''Who? Lucky to find who?'' He helped himself to a large slice of EttaMae's cake, and then made himself comfortable next to Big Daddy at the table.

Big Daddy gave his nephew an affable pat on the back. ''We were just talkin' about what a gold mine Syd is for Montana.''

''A veritable match made in heaven,'' Tex agreed, a minxish curl to his upper lip. ''Together, they are a well-oiled machine. Kind of like a good marriage, in a way. All the guys say so.'' Montana kicked his brother under the table and, shoulders bobbing, Tex dived into his cake.

''Well, good. That's what I like to hear.''

Casting a warning glance at his idiot brother, Montana opted to change the subject. ''Big Daddy, I have been meaning to talk to you about taking a more proactive stance toward our drought management efforts. I've been keeping an eye on the weather report, and I don't see any signs that it's going to let up in the near future. I believe we need to start thinking about some damage control.''

''I'm all ears. Whatcha got in mind?''

''I think we should sell off some of the cattle.''

''Which ones?''

''Right now, we've got about four or five hundred head out in section ten. The stream out there is starting to dry up and the cow tanks we've got in that section won't help much in this heat. Plus, I'm really worried about overgrazing, blackleg, parasites, heel flies.'' Montana let his fork clatter to his plate. ''You name it, and I'm worried about it.''

The occasional chink of a horseshoe hitting the metal

post, followed by hoots of laughter from the guys, drew Montana's gaze. At times like this, he was ready to relinquish his foreman position to Tex and go to work for his father in the corporate business world. He could always dabble with a little spread of his own, in his spare time.

"Don't worry, son. I know you're doing your best. Sometimes in the ranching bidness, ya take a hit or two." The old man's face stretched into a pliant smile of understanding. "That's what we got oil rigs for. To take up the financial slack. You do what you gotta do. If it doesn't rain pretty soon, you might even have to cut out a few more 'n that. You gonna go get 'em tomorrow?"

"The sooner the better."

"Right. Who you taking with you?"

Like a magnet to steel, Montana's gaze honed in on Sydney. "I was thinking of taking the Kid."

"I'll go," Tex volunteered.

Montana snorted.

"Fine." Big Daddy stood. "Speaking of going...I gotta get." He patted Montana on the shoulder. "The three of you and a few dogs should be all ya need. Take horses. It's so tinder dry out there, the ATVs could start a fire. A gas leak or a spark would be all we'd need. Just don't want to take any chances. Anywho, if you start early, you can have 'em back here in the holdin' area for inspection by late afternoon. Call me when you get back."

After shouting a few effusive goodbyes, the old man was gone.

Montana glared at Tex. "Remind me that we still have to beat you up after everyone leaves."

Tex threw back his head and laughed.

Sydney couldn't remember ever having a nicer day. As she readied herself for bed that night, she thought back to the pancakes, the lazy drive through the countryside, the rodeo and even the barbecue that evening. Everything with Montana was so much fun. Even when his younger brother was making a complete pest of himself, something in Montana's supercharged gaze made her feel as if they were alone.

A light T-shirt and a pair of shorts was all she needed for pajamas, even with the cooling breeze from the air conditioner. Once she'd tidied everything and set out her clothes for work in the morning, she snapped off her bedside lamp. After her eyes adjusted, she found she could still see quite well. Must be the gorgeous full moon they'd enjoyed all evening. She moved to the window to enjoy the sight as it hovered overhead.

It really was a beautiful setting, actually, this little grouping of cabins nestled in amongst the trees at the edge of the pond. Although the pond didn't seem nearly as expansive as it had on the day she arrived. The water used to come to the underbelly of the dock. Now the dock stuck up out of the water, like a spindly-legged flamingo.

Feeling restless, Sydney unlocked her window and threw up the sash. Immediately the soulful sound of cricket song greeted her. That, and a sudden and unusual hissing sound. Snake? No. She cocked her head. Snakes wouldn't be out hissing around after midnight, would they?

"Pssssst!"

Sydney's head jerked around, and after she took a moment to force her heart back out of her throat, a smile lit her face. Montana was hanging out of his own bedroom window and waving at her. The ten-foot width of the bathroom was all that separated them.

"Hi! What are you doing?" she whispered over to him, feeling suddenly giddy.

"I was looking at the moon, but now I'm coming to visit

you.'' With a grunt, he hefted himself out of his window and landed with a thud on the dry ground below. "Uff. I'm gonna kill him," he muttered.

"Are you okay?"

"Think so." Upon standing, he dusted himself off and picked his way—shirtless, barefoot and wearing only a pair of jeans—to her window.

On tiptoe, Sydney strained out the window toward him. The sill dug into her ribs, but she didn't care. When he came into her arms, warm and smooth, rock hard and smelling like spicy shampoo and deodorant and mouthwash, all other minor inconveniences dwindled into little specks of nothing. This was where she belonged. She was becoming more sure of that with each breath she took. Her nose bumped into his neck as his powerful arms surrounded her waist. Leaning back, he searched for her mouth with his own.

"Hi," he whispered against her lips before giving her the long, slow, sweet kiss that she'd been thinking of all evening.

"Hi, yourself."

"Mmm. This is nice."

"It would be nicer if your brother wasn't sprawled out on the floor between our rooms, forcing you to sneak around like some kind of fugitive from justice." She allowed her head to drop back so that he could have better access to that spot on her neck that he knew just how to kiss. "Although—" she sighed lazily "—meeting like this does have a certain charm."

"I thought all those bozos would never go home."

"Me, too. They'd still be out there playing if you hadn't shooed everyone off. I think EttaMae's cake gave them all a sugar buzz."

"Probably. I know you're giving me one."

"Mmm. Very clever."

He withdrew his arms from her waist and cupped her face in his hands and, angling her mouth to his, kissed her senseless for a while. Heart hammering, Sydney clutched his smooth, muscular shoulders, and reveled in the onslaught. This was so wonderful. So magical. And yet, she yearned for a normal relationship. How much longer could she continue to live in this shroud of secrecy? At the moment, she didn't think she could last another day. She wanted everyone to share in their happiness.

"By the way…" Montana settled his hands at her hips and rubbed his nose against hers. "Tomorrow you are working with me all day. We'll be herding some cattle back from section ten."

She smiled. "That's wonderful."

"Tex is coming."

"That's horrible."

Frustrated, Montana exhaled noisily. "I know."

"Can we ditch him?"

"We can try."

"But I wouldn't count on it." The sardonic tone of Tex's voice reached them just before the blinding beam of a flashlight.

Squinting against the light, Montana scowled. "What the hell are you doing out here?"

"Just doin' my job, brother dear. I don't make the rules around here. I just enforce 'em." He focused on Sydney with the light. "Hey, Kid."

Sydney shielded her eyes with her hand. "You know, we were supposed to beat him up after everyone left, weren't we?"

"How could we have let that opportunity slip by?"

Tex guffawed. "Just got busy doing other things, from the look of it."

"I vote we do it now." Montana held out his arms and lifted Sydney to the ground.

"Oh, now, wait just a minute, I have bare feet," Tex complained as he began to back away.

"Then we're even. Better hoof it, little brother, because when we catch you, you're going to be sorry."

"You guys are sickening."

"I don't recall asking you along," Montana told Tex as they rode their horses out to section ten, bright and early the next morning. Saddle leather squeaked as Montana turned in his seat and pulled Sydney a little closer. Unfazed, Geranium edged ever closer to Bullet, and clip-clopped placidly along the dusty road. Fingers twined, their hands swayed to the gentle rhythm of the horses' gait. "Did you invite him?"

"Heck, no. Although—" she lifted a teasing brow "—maybe a bodyguard isn't such a bad idea." They'd been flirting outrageously ever since they'd left the view of the ranch offices, and Sydney was feeling as ebullient as a puppy.

Montana arched a rakish brow. "I just love it when you threaten me with bodily harm."

"Yeesh." Tex grimaced. "Here we go again."

"Brother, there are advantages to dating a cowboy."

"I don't date co-workers. Unless they look like her."

"This one's taken, brother."

"I know. I know."

The possessive note in Montana's voice thrilled Sydney from the top of her hat to the tips of her boots. Their eyes met for a moment, and the message exchanged was a silent promise. Later. They would find a few minutes alone.

The sun was already blazing hot and it wasn't even midmorning yet. Billows of dust, churned up by the horses' hooves, swirled in their wake. For as far as the eye could see in all directions in the endless expanse of the azure Texas sky, no cloud could be found. Three cow dogs, Roo-roo, Woof and Badluck—an unfortunate creature who'd lost an ear in a run-in with a bull—trotted alongside the horses, tongues lolling in an effort to stay cool.

Section ten was out near the western border of Big Daddy's ranch, and the ride there took longer than usual because of the incredible heat. Ten was the best grazing section they had at the moment for cattle in drought conditions. The pasture there hadn't been overgrazed yet. Besides the cow tanks, the stream—such as it was—ran through a wooded gully, affording at least some relief from the weather. However, when they finally arrived, after a seemingly endless trek, Montana's worst fears were confirmed. The stream had narrowed down to a creeklike trickle in a matter of a day or two.

They all dismounted to inspect the giant cracks in the mud around the stream's banks—a gentle slope on one side, and a steep bank on the other. The mesquite and juniper trees that grew here were dry and brittle, having been scorched by the sun and withered by lack of rainfall.

Montana thumbed his hat back and shook his head. "Not that long ago, the stream bed was ten times this wide. More like a small river."

It was only slightly cooler in the shade, and they paused to rest and let their mounts drink for a bit, before they got started rounding up the cattle. A large percentage of the herd was right there, trying to stay out of the sun. Some were lying down, others stood motionless. All heads slowly swiveled to level curious stares at the newcomers. Some of the cattle took a few steps of approach. Some hung back. All looked as if they'd already been barbecued.

For about an hour they all worked together, using the

dogs to channel the listless cattle into the shady box-shaped gully where Montana would count them before they started back to the holding pen behind the stables. It was hard, dusty work, but all things considered, they made good time. By noon, as near as Montana could figure, they'd rounded up nearly four hundred head. That left between fifty and a hundred stragglers grazing in other quadrants of the section to round up before they could begin driving them back home. Finding those animals would take some time.

After a quick sandwich, eaten in a shady area near the stream's rocky shore, Montana, Sydney and Tex doused their hats and handkerchiefs in water and were back at work.

Montana whistled for Woof, and Sydney paused to watch as he and the dog hustled a stray away from the fence line. "Go get 'em, Woof. Right. Right again. Left. Good dog. Bring 'em in. Let's go, Woof. Atta boy." An invisible signal to his horse had him turning around. Pounding through the dust, Montana headed the confused steer off and got him going in the right direction.

Sydney sighed as she watched. The sky was so big and blue, the grass so golden and Montana…well, Montana, like the cowboys of old, was poetry in motion.

Tex caught up with his brother and, leaning forward in his saddle, listened for Montana's direction. They reined in their mounts and, deep in discussion, nodded together and pointed along the fence line.

Eventually, as if he could sense that she watched, Montana lifted his eyes and his gaze collided with hers in that high-voltage connection that passed between the two of them with growing frequency.

Never had she been so glad to be a woman.

Tex was the first to strike out away from the gully. Whistling for Badluck, he shouted, "I'll check the south fence for strays. You guys want to stay north of the stream?''

"What, and leave me alone with this woman? What about the safety of my body?" The sarcasm in Montana's voice was comical.

"I'll just have to trust that you can fend her off for the next hour, without me."

Sydney waggled a brow. "I'll be gentle with him."

Tex grinned. "See ya."

Montana swung back into his saddle and crossed to the north side of the stream. "I'll start on this end, you head up over there, and we'll drive back that way."

Sydney glanced back to the areas he indicated and nodded. "Okay. Come on, Roo."

From where the affable cow dog stood in the stream, he perked his ears. For an uncustomary moment, he hung back, then seeming to decide he had no choice, bounded out of the water and followed Sydney.

Sydney reined Geranium around and headed to the northeast. Montana and Woof headed northwest. The sun blazed down from the sky and Sydney thought that she'd never been in such heat. Sweat poured in rivulets between her shoulder blades, and her hat felt as if it was on fire. Each time she rounded several of the outlying herd back toward the gully, she'd urge Geranium and Roo into what was left of the stream for a refreshing splash, and then head back out for more cattle.

Off in the distance, she could see Montana prodding a few sluggish beasts into action. He'd call for Woof and the spunky animal would do his best, but even the dogs seemed to be succumbing to the extraordinary heat.

One torturous hour dragged into another.

Tex had ridden down the south fence line and was now

completely out of sight. Montana was nearer, but still too far for conversation.

As Sydney and Geranium clip-clopped up a jagged hill that seemed to be made of solid slate, she wondered at the surface temperature. No doubt she could fry an egg. She could probably fry bacon on these rocks. In fact, she'd be willing to bet that if she stuck a chicken on a stick, she could roast it. Pausing in her ascent, she wiped her brow on the back of her sleeve. She felt like a chicken on a stick. Sizzling.

Hmm. All this thinking about food made her stomach growl. It had been several hours since lunch. She must be hungry. Either that or delirious. Lord knew she was thirsty.

Oh, it was hot.

Kiln hot.

As Geranium's hooves struck the rock, Sydney could almost envision sparks flying. Sydney thought about telling Montana that they should call it a day. That it was too hot out here. But then he'd think she was a wimp.

Not to mention the fact that they'd probably lose all of these cattle if they didn't get them out of here before the sun rose too much higher in the sky. It had been hot over the past weeks, but nothing like this.

As Sydney neared the top of the rocky bluff, she heard the bawling of a young calf coming from amongst some boulders and scrub brush. Drawing near, she could see that a calf had somehow slipped into a tight crevasse between two boulders.

"How did you get down there, little guy?" Sydney could see that he was wedged. Eyes rolled back in its head, front feet flailing, the calf struggled to free itself. "You got yourself stuck in there pretty tight, huh?" Sydney sighed. Getting this calf loose would take more than just two hands and a rope.

She called for Montana. At first he didn't hear her above the din of the bawling cattle, so she waved and finally caught his eye.

"Whatcha got?" he wondered as he rode up.

"This little guy is stuck all the way up to his armpits," she explained. "I thought about trying to pull him out, but without someone to brace him, I was afraid I'd tear him in two."

"Yeah. I see what you mean."

Montana handed his reins to Sydney and got off his horse to inspect. "You are really stuck, little buddy."

"I wonder how he got down there?" Sydney dismounted and tethered both horses to the brittle branches of a scrubby-looking bush.

"Must have fallen down the hill." He squinted up. "Maybe something spooked him."

"How long do you think he's been there?" She crouched down next to where he sat on his haunches.

"Not too long. Couldn't live between these rocks for too long in this heat."

"Where's Tex?"

"Still on the south fence, I guess. He'll probably be gone for a while longer."

"That would be a first."

Montana laughed. "Hand me that rope, will you?" He gestured to the lasso that hung from his saddle horn.

Sydney brought him the rope.

"Sure is hazy all of a sudden." Sydney looked around.

"Yeah."

"Think we'll get some rain?"

"Wouldn't count on it."

"Here, take this." He handed her the other end of the rope and gestured to Geranium. "When I give the signal, back up. Slowly."

"Okay." Sydney took her end of the rope and, after mounting Geranium, wrapped it around her saddle horn and waited for the signal. The air had an odd quality, suddenly heavy. Geranium pranced a bit and shook his head. Sydney had to force her usually docile mount to stay put. "What's wrong with you? Settle down."

"You ready?" Montana grunted, straddling the calf and gripping it behind its front legs.

"Kind of."

"Is that a yes?"

"Yes." Slowly she backed her skittish mount up, and within minutes the calf was free of the crevasse. No sooner had Montana pulled the rope from around its body than it was limping off, dragging a hind leg and bawling for its mother.

A subtle change in the oven-hot breeze carried the faint scent of smoke to Sydney's nose. She urged the wary Geranium up the hill to get a better view of the western horizon.

"Uh, Montana?" As Sydney squinted off into the distance, a feeling of foreboding grabbed hold of her gut and a surge of adrenaline left her feeling light-headed.

"Yeah?"

Her body felt heavy and her tongue unwieldy in her suddenly dry mouth. "I…I…think I see what it is that spooked our little buddy."

Montana pulled off his leather gloves and wiped his brow on his sleeve. "What?"

"Fire," she croaked, turning the prancing Geranium around and pounding back down the hill to where Montana stood. "A big fire," she shouted, "and it looks like it's headed this way."

Chapter Ten

"Damn."

Montana swung into his saddle and rode up to the crest of the hill. Jawline granite, he stared for a moment before galloping back to her side. Frustrated beyond endurance, he cursed roundly. "This is the last thing we need."

"What do you think started it?"

"Could be any number of things."

"What should we do?"

"Find Tex, and get the hell out of here."

"From the angle of the plumbs of smoke, looks like there's a tail wind pushing the fire this way, don't you think?"

"Yep." Again he swore under his breath and motioned for her to follow. "It's comin' from the southwest."

"Where Tex is?" It was more of a statement than a question.

"Probably." Montana nodded. "Come on. Grass fires eat up the acreage fast. We don't have much time. I'm just guessing, but I bet we only have about fifteen, maybe twenty minutes before it's here, unless the winds change. Let's get started.''

"What about the cattle?''

"Nothing we can do," he shouted over his shoulder, already urging Bullet away from the oncoming fire and back toward the stream. "We can try to get them to stampede out of the gully and set them on track for home, but I don't think we should hang around to drive 'em. With any luck, some of 'em will make it.''

Sydney wanted to cry. So many of the cattle in this section were calves.

They spent the next frantic minutes searching the south side of the stream for Tex, to no avail. The smoke was getting heavier by the second, drying out Sydney's mouth and stinging her eyes.

"*Tex!*'' she screamed, her throat raw. "*Tex!* Answer me!'' She could hear Montana shouting off in the distance, but there was nothing from Tex.

Ravenous flames that devoured acres of tinder-dry grass as if it were a pre-entrée appetizer roared toward them with terrifying speed. But they couldn't leave without Tex. Cattle, having sensed the imminent danger, had already begun to mill about and bawl.

Visibility was beginning to wane. Montana appeared before her through a hazy smog and Sydney was weak with relief at the sight of him.

"I can't find Tex," she sobbed, and urged the less than cooperative Geranium back toward Montana.

"You go," Montana commanded, riding up and taking her by the arm. "Head back toward the offices. Get help. I'll stay and look for Tex.''

"I'm not leaving without you.''

"No. I don't want you out here. It's too dangerous.''

"I'm not leaving without you.''

"No! Sydney, I said go."

"Haven't I proved anything to you yet? Why do you still treat me like a helpless ninny? Dammit, Montana, if you are staying, I'm staying!" Her eyes filled with tears. "I can't leave without knowing that you're going to be okay. Do you understand?"

Montana looked deep into her eyes for a moment, seeming to weigh the sincerity of her words. "Okay. Come on."

Calling to the dogs, they rode over to where the cattle huddled in the gully and, whips cracking, started to drive them out. Sydney echoed Montana's shouts until she was hoarse. Luckily, Roo, Geranium, Woof and Montana seemed to sense and second-guess her every move, and together they had the cattle running pell-mell down the road in the general direction of the holding pen outside the stables. Woof and Roo were hot on their hooves, barking and nipping at the haunches of those who got confused in the haze.

Montana and Sydney watched them depart. Whether or not they would ever arrive was anybody's guess.

Turning back toward the fire, they used up more precious moments, searching once again—and still unsuccessfully—for Tex. The heat and smoke were becoming unbearable.

"He's not here," Montana finally shouted. He rode up next to her. "I'm guessing he couldn't find us while we were freeing that calf. Maybe he figured we saw the fire and left."

"I wish we could be sure."

"Me, too."

By this time, the fire had whipped over section eleven and was now encroaching upon ten. It jumped from tree to tree, shooting down the banks of the stream and making it impossible to cross back to the south side.

"Let's go back. Head north," Montana shouted, to be heard above the inferno, but his words were unnecessary.

Sydney was at his side as they rode, just ahead of the fire, back toward the areas they'd been working that morning, and beyond. Smoke swirled around, slowing their progress, and branches crashed to the ground behind them, spooking the horses.

And still, there was no sign of Tex.

"Which way?" Sydney cried over her shoulder when they came to a fork in the road.

"Stay left. Just keep bearing north and I think we'll make it. The smoke doesn't seem quite as bad over here. Maybe the fire is staying south of us." Montana pulled ahead of her and looked around. "This side of the stream seems okay so far. Let's stick to the road and try to stay away from the trees."

She did. The road was rutted and the terrain fraught with jutting hills and sudden valleys on this side of the stream, making the going more difficult.

"Montana!"

"Yeah?"

"There's a big pile of rocks in the middle of the road up ahead." Pulling closer, she could see that these boulders had rolled, avalanche-style, down the hill. "Should I go up or down?"

"Down. Going up is too dangerous. Rocks look loose."

"Okay."

Slowly they picked their way around the boulders and found the road again.

And there, on the other side of the rocks, sitting loyally in the middle of the road, was Badluck. Tail wagging, he began barking excitedly when he saw them approach.

"Badluck!" Sydney's heart leapt into her throat as she

reached down and scratched his good ear. What was Tex's dog still doing out here?

"Where is he, boy? Where is Tex?" Montana jumped off his horse and followed the dog back toward the rocks. "Sydney! Over here."

She dismounted and, rushing after Montana, found Tex lying on the ground, his leg pinned by a boulder. He was conscious, but rummy.

"He's got a pretty nasty cut on the back of his head," Montana told Sydney as he stripped off his shirt and used it to stem the flow of his brother's blood. "We're gonna need some help."

"Can we move him?"

"Not without some tools and about a half dozen extra pairs of hands."

Sydney crouched down next to Montana and patted Tex's arm. "Tex? Can you hear me?"

"I hear angels," he murmured. "Am I in heaven?"

Montana snorted as he tied his shirt securely around Tex's head. "Some bodyguard you turned out to be."

A weak, lopsided grin pushed at Tex's lips. "I'm still on the job. It's hard to fool around with her when I'm lying here bleeding to death."

"You're not going to bleed to death. We won't let you."

"Oh, sure. You guys are probably…gonna try and beat me up."

"Later." Montana winked at Sydney. "What happened?"

Voice high and breathy, Tex gave his hands a limp wave. "It was the damnedest thing. I was over here…looking for you guys, when a little calf came limping along. It was…bawling…something fierce." Tex grimaced as obvious pains shot through his leg. "So I lassoed him, climbed off…my horse and was checkin' him over and the next thing I know a bunch of stampeding cattle is knocking boulders over that bluff.'' He pointed woozily behind his head. "Didn't...have time to get out of the way, I guess. Damned horse ran off.''

Montana felt for his brother's pulse as he spoke to Sydney under his breath. "I need you to ride back to the ranch offices and get help.''

"I'm on my way.''

Before Montana had time to digest her response, Sydney had mounted Geranium and was headed down the road. "Don't worry,'' she called over her shoulder. "I'll bring back help. You won't even know I'm gone. Trust me.''

"I do,'' he called after her retreating form, only to discover that for the first time in years, when it came to a woman, he really and truly did.

Lying down nearly jockey-style, Sydney soared down the road on Geranium's back, at breakneck speeds. The wind ruffled her hair and billowed her shirt, cooling her slightly. The smoke was much less dense, the closer she got to the ranch offices. Finally, after what seemed an eternity, Sydney came tearing into the paddock.

She leapt from her horse's back before he came to a complete stop and staggered headlong around the stables and into the ranch offices, screaming like a banshee the whole while.

"Big Daddy! Fuzzy! Red! Somebody! Anybody!''

BettyJean was not at her desk, so Sydney barreled past and blew into Big Daddy's office. With a bang, the door slammed open and the startled man looked up from a Platt map that he'd been studying and stared.

Sydney fell against the door frame and gasped for air. "Big Daddy! There's...oh...there's—'' She pointed out the window behind him and struggled to regain her composure.

"What is it, darlin'?" Big Daddy rushed to her side and led her to a chair. "Take it easy now, lamb chop, and tell me what's going on."

"It's…Tex," she panted, feeling faint. "There's a fire…out there. Big, big fire. A boulder fell…Tex is pinned. Montana is with him."

"Gotcha." Big Daddy reached for the phone and the radio at the same time. On the phone, he ordered fire and medical assistance. On the radio, he called for the hands, who came barreling into the office before he could sign off. Reaching into his desk, he grabbed a bottle of pricey whiskey and tossed it to Fuzzy. "Colt, you go round up some blankets. Kenny, grab the first aid kit. Red, get a couple buckets of fresh water, the rest of you go get my Land Rover and load it with crowbars, shovels, pickaxes, whatever you can get your hands on. Everyone meet out front in three minutes and pile in. Syd will show us the way."

All hands scrambled to obey Big Daddy's curt commands and the next three minutes were a blur to Sydney as they loaded the Land Rover with necessary supplies. In a complete daze, she climbed into Big Daddy's rig and, praying all the while, led her impromptu army on an interminable, jouncing journey around a stampeding herd of cattle, past two hardworking dogs, across a shriveling stream and out to the burning battlefield.

It wasn't until they'd entered the swirling vortex of thick, black smoke and nearly collided with a pile of boulders that Sydney realized Big Daddy had called her lamb chop.

When Sydney leapt out of the Land Rover and ran straight into his arms, Montana had never been so happy to see anyone in his life. He pulled her up against his body and kissed her hard on the mouth.

"I was getting worried," he confessed. "It got so smoky, I couldn't tell where the fire was." He pointed back toward the stream. "I think we'll be okay here for a little while, anyway. The fire seems to still be heading south."

"I know, I know, thank God," she murmured against his lips. "I couldn't stand riding so far away from you, wondering if you and Tex were all right out here. How is he?"

"I think he'll be okay. Thanks to you." Again he kissed her soundly.

As the men poured out of the Land Rover they all stopped and stared, stupefied.

Montana looked up and noticed their stunned expressions and laughed. "What's the matter, you never see a foreman kiss his assistant before?"

Red turned a blistering shade of fuchsia, and Fuzzy looked a little green under his whiskers.

"I hate to interrupt, but could somebody please give me a hand over here?"

The sound of Tex's tinny voice spurred everyone into action and, jaws slack, they fumbled about unloading tools and then stumbled in shock to Tex's side. Soon they had the boulder leveraged away from his leg and he was able to pull it free. And—save for some pretty nasty black-and-blue marks—his leg was no worse for the wear. With some assistance, Tex limped back to the Land Rover and after everyone piled back in, Big Daddy started the engine and roared back to the safety of his house.

A half hour later, as helicopters thundered overhead to battle the grass fire that was blessedly moving farther and farther south, everyone gathered in Big Daddy's office for a celebratory drink. Dust covered and smelling like smoke, the cowboys reclined on the plentiful fine leather upholstery and congratulated each other on a job well done.

Especially the Kid.

Seated on Montana's lap and glad to finally be open about the true nature of their relationship, she ducked her head and shrugged off their praises by changing the subject.

"Okay, tell me the truth. You mean to tell me that not one of you guys ever once guessed that I might be a girl?"

"I didn't know you were a gal," Fuzzy confessed. "I just thought you was a real goofy-lookin' boy. Kinda too purty to be natural. But you worked so dang hard, and you're so good at what you do, I just, I don't know, I guess I just thought puberty would eventually cure ya. Did you know she was a gal, Red?"

Blushing madly, Red shook his head. "Nope. But I did think she was strange."

Colt hooted. "I didn't think you were any guy. Me and Kenny knew you were a girl from the second we laid eyes on you. Willie, too. Right, guys?"

Kenny and Willie shook their heads. "Baloney, Colt. You thought she was a goofy little guy, just like the rest of us."

Sydney grinned, surprised to find that she was not offended in the least. Her gaze traveled to Big Daddy. "You knew all along, didn't you?"

Big Daddy nodded, his weathered face wreathed in smile lines.

"But you let her share a bunkhouse with me anyway?" Montana asked, incredulous.

"Yep. I had Tex lookin' out for ya. With him doggin' ya, I knew you'd stay out of trouble."

Montana rolled his eyes.

"If you knew," Sydney asked, "then why did you hire me?"

"Honey pie, I figured that anyone who was willin' to cut off that gorgeous mane of hair and come out here and work her fingers to the bone had to be someone worth hiring. And I figured as long as no one was making a big stink about you being a woman, and you fit in all right, then you could stay." Angling his head, he grinned at Montana. "Besides, I know a match made in heaven when I see one."

"You sure do, Big Daddy." Montana's head slowly bobbed. "You sure do."

"I wish you didn't have to go." Montana heaved a forlorn sigh.

Sydney cradled his face in the palms of her hands. "I know. I wish I didn't have to go, either. But now that everyone knows I'm a woman, I have to move out. It's the rule."

They'd left Big Daddy's office over an hour ago, and were now fresh out of the shower and wearing clean shorts and T-shirts. Together they lounged on the living-room couch in front of a portable air-conditioning unit that Montana had brought in from the stable's storeroom. The fire was under control, as of the last report, and wouldn't be coming anywhere near the bunkhouses, or Big Daddy's mansion.

"You don't have to move out." Montana nuzzled her neck and Sydney giggled.

"Yes, I do, you naughty boy. I'm surprised that Big Daddy didn't intervene long before this."

"He knows I'm a gentleman." He nibbled her ear. "Don't move. Stay."

"Some gentleman."

"We could work around Big Daddy's rules."

"How?"

Montana stopped cold in his ministrations and pulled

back. There was a look in his eyes she'd never seen before. A look of boyish vulnerability that had her heart climbing into her mouth. Very slowly he took her hands in his and cleared his throat. "You could stay, if you married me."

Sydney's pulse began to sing in her ears and she was suddenly filled with an incredible joy. "Marry you?" she whispered.

"Say yes. I love you, Sydney MacKenzie. But even more important than that…" He paused and pressed her fingers to his lips. "I trust you. With my life. With my future. Please say you'll be my wife."

Uncontrolled, tears welled in her eyes and hovered at her lower lashes. "Yes! Yes, I'll marry you. I love you, too, Montana Brubaker," she whispered, her emotion making her words halting. "And, more important—" the tears spilled over her lashes and began to stream down her cheeks "—I can't think of anyone I'd rather have for a partner in this life."

Sighing with relief and happiness, Montana pulled Sydney into his arms and kissed her soundly.

Directly behind them, the front door flew open and Tex's voice reached them. "Hi, guys. The paramedics got me all outfitted with some swanky new crutches, and I thought I'd try 'em out by swinging by your place for a chat. You know, now that everyone knows Syd is a woman, you guys probably shouldn't—"

Reaching behind his head, Montana gave the front door a shove. Its resounding slam cut Tex off midsentence.

"Ahhh. Blessed peace and quiet," he murmured, drawing Sydney's face back into his palms. "Now. Where were we?"

"I believe we were right about—" Sydney pulled his lower lip into her mouth and nibbled "—here."

"And so we were."

Epilogue

Six months later

Everyone said that Sydney MacKenzie made the most beautiful bride anyone had ever seen, and her husband of less than an hour couldn't agree more. Big Daddy had insisted on hosting their spectacular wedding in his rose garden, telling them that it was becoming family tradition.

As Montana led Sydney around the dance floor, the throngs of well-wishers seemed to fade into the background.

"I got you a wedding present," he told her, looking into the incredible emerald of her eyes. "But I couldn't wrap him."

"Him?" Sydney tilted her chin. "You got me a puppy!"

"Kind of. Would you like to see?"

"Yes!"

Taking her by the hand, Montana tugged her away from the dance floor, through the rose garden, around the mas-

CAROLYN ZANE 179

sive Brubaker mansion and to the circular drive. There, parked by the fountain, was Montana's truck. Behind it was a trailer containing a massive bull.

"Roger!" Sydney squealed upon spying his horns, and threw herself into Montana's arms. "How did you get him?"

"Told the new owner your story. You know, about how hard your papa worked, and you on the verge of losing your company and all. Didn't want to sell to me at first, but his wife was a softy and twisted his arm."

"Oh, how wonderful!" Her eyes brimmed with tears of happiness as she traced his jaw with trembling fingertips. "My father would be so pleased."

"I'm glad." He kissed her nose. "I figure we can keep him here until we finish remodeling your house. Then we can move out to your place and old Roger there can get started on his family."

"Just as long as he doesn't beat us to the punch."

"Mmm. Woman, I love the way your mind works. What say we skip the rest of this celebration and head straight to the honeymoon?"

Behind them, Tex's voice rang out. "Oh, hey, there you are! I've been looking everywhere. It's time for me to toast—"

"Quick! Let's go!" Sydney hiked her skirts and dived into the driver's side of Montana's truck.

Hot on her heels, Montana shoved her over, started the engine and careered down the driveway, a bewildered Roger Ramjet bawling from the trailer.

"Think they'll let him on the cruise ship?" Sydney wondered, laughing.

"We'll probably have to pay extra for a bigger room, but it will be worth it, if it means escaping Tex."

Their happy laughter—coupled with Roger's indignant squawks—could be heard wafting on the breeze as Montana made good his escape with his feisty cowgirl bride.

* * * * * *

Carolyn Zane has plenty more
romances in store for that
brood of Brubaker boys.

Turn the page for a
sneak peak at the latest book in

THE BRUBAKER BRIDES
series...

TEX'S EXASPERATING HEIRESS

on sale

January 2001
from Silhouette Romance

Chapter One

Charlotte Beauchamp was stuck with a real pig.

Not as the word might pertain to a chauvinistic man. Nor a pig, as some might use the word to describe a broken-down car, an overly enthusiastic law officer or a ravenous, somewhat slovenly dinner companion.

No, Charlotte Beauchamp was stuck with a *real* pig.

The farm-animal variety, turned indoor pet. A potbellied number that snorted, rolled in mud whenever it got the chance and ate a nauseating mixture of leftovers—commonly referred to as "slop"—for breakfast.

"Pardon me?" Miss Clarise Brubaker, Charlotte's second cousin—once removed—was obviously taken aback. "When Aunt Dorothy died, she did what?"

Charlotte sighed. "She left me a pig."

Miss Clarise and Big Daddy, her husband of over forty years, exchanged incredulous glances.

"A...pig."

"Yes, ma'am."

"Just a pig?"

"For now, yes."

The three were seated in the parlor of the Brubakers' opulent Texas mansion. Though they were only distant relatives, the well-known oil baron and his wife always made Charlotte feel as though she were part of the gargantuan Brubaker family that included nine offspring, their spouses and children, and a host of nieces and nephews. There was something so infinitely loveable about the millionaire munchkin, Big Daddy, and his sweet wife, Miss Clarise.

"My aunt Dorothy left you a pig?" With a clatter, Miss Clarise set her teacup on the silver tray in front of her and struggled to keep her soft-spoken drawl…soft. "But, sweetheart, as her great-granddaughter, and considering your lovely parents have passed on to glory, *you* were her only living heir! And, darlin', your Nanna Dorothy was rich!"

"Filthy rich," Big Daddy put in.

"I can't believe she could be so cruel. Especially considering that you gave up your personal life to nurse her for the last ten of her hundred years. Surely you can contest this will. Quite clearly, she wasn't in her right mind when she left you a…a…*pig!*"

"Well, actually, Miss Clarise, in a roundabout way she did leave everything to me. You see, within the will there is a proviso that states I must 'adopt,' for lack of a better word, Toto and raise him as if he were my own child."

"Toto?"

"The pig."

"I…see." Miss Clarise simply stared.

"Yes. Very soon Nanna Dorothy's estate will be sold and the proceeds put into a trust account with the rest of her assets. I'll inherit everything if—and only if—I promise to love, honor and obey the—" she wrinkled her nose at the thought of the despicable animal ''—uh…Toto for the rest of his life.''

She cast a thousand-watt smile upon Miss Clarise, who had been a Beauchamp before she married Big Daddy. "To be perfectly honest, I'm not worried about inheriting the money. If it happens, fine. If not, I'll make do somehow. I just hope I can live through the next few years without honey-glazing Toto and serving him for Christmas dinner. Which brings me to one of the reasons I'm here, aside from visiting the two of you.''

Turning in her seat, Charlotte faced Big Daddy. "I understand through Toto's vet that one of your nephews is named Tex?''

"Yes, we have a nephew 'at goes by Tex. Lives here on the Circle BO. One of my brother's boys.''

"Great. I hear that Tex has an excellent reputation as an animal trainer. Especially farm animals. They say he can turn even the most savage beast into a docile little lamb.''

Big Daddy nodded. "That's our Tex. Ever since he was knee-high to a toadstool, that kid could break the mustangs. He's also great with cow dogs. He's got a growing practice that he's building right here on the ranch, out beyond the stable apiece. Went to school, came out with a fistful of degrees and now he does a lot of research for the university in his clinic.'' Charlotte couldn't help but smile. Big Daddy was so obviously proud of his nephew. "It's a pretty big deal,'' the older man continued. "Tex's what they call an animal behaviorist.''

"Oh? Hmmm. I think I might need more of an animal exorcist.'' Charlotte exhaled and dropped her head back against the lush sofa cushion. "I'm reasonably certain that Toto is possessed.''

"I'm certain Tex will be happy to take Toto on as a client,'' Miss Clarise assured her.

Perhaps Miss Clarise spoke too soon, Charlotte mused. Or perhaps the fates were against her. Perhaps the disgusting, madcap Toto was Satan's spawn whose sole destiny was to make her life a living hell. Because, as they sipped from fine china cups, filled with aromatic Darjeeling tea, and nibbled on delicate lady fingers, the ugly, salivating, whirling dervish that was Toto came barreling into the parlor.

Hot on the renegade Toto's hooves, a glowering cowboy thundered into the parlor and skidded to a stop just shy of the sofa. He gave a deferential nod in Charlotte's direction before he spoke.

"Miss Clarise, Big Daddy, I'm sorry to interrupt your little visit, but I found this poor pig locked in a car outside. Some moron left him to die."

Charlotte frowned as she jumped to her feet. *Moron?* Insulted, she shot the buttinski ranch hand a withering glance before she darted off after the lawless Toto, who was now running amuck at the other end of the expansive parlor.

"Oh, Miss Clarise, I'm…so terribly sorry…that my pig got…out…." Charlotte huffed and lunged for the bristly missile as he headed back to where they'd all been sitting. His curly tail slipped through her fingertips as he dived under the table that held the delicate tea service. "I'll…pay…for any…damage…that he—" again Toto dodged her grasp "—that he…might do."

"*Your* pig?" The ranch hand thumbed his Stetson back and smirked.

"Yes." Charlotte grunted and yanked Toto from under the table by his collar, but not before he upset a cup of tea and sent its contents raining onto the Turkish rug.

"No, no, Toto!" she cried. Dropping to her knees, she

picked up the broken porcelain cup. "I'm so very sorry. Usually he doesn't act quite this badly."

"Probably because you keep him locked in a car," the ranch hand roared.

Charlotte hauled herself to her feet and stood swaying. With murder in her eye, she dragged her hair out of her face and stared at this boar. Obviously it took one to know one. "The door was *un*locked."

Tex snorted his disgust. "Oh, now that's helpful. For a *cloven-hoofed beast!*"

"I parked in the shade!"

"The shade moved," the cowboy bit out, his eyes steely.

"I left the engine in my car running and the air-conditioning on."

"You ran out of gas."

"Toto, no!" Charlotte looked helplessly at Miss Clarise as Toto crashed into a china cabinet loaded with priceless bric-a-brac. "I don't know why he's acting this way."

The cowboy smirked. "It's clear why he's acting this way."

At the boiling point, Charlotte stopped and stared. "Who *are* you?"

Miss Clarise jumped to her feet, her soft Southern drawl giving this ridiculous situation an element of class. "Charlotte, dear, allow me to introduce you to my nephew on Big Daddy's side, Tex Brubaker. Tex, this is Charlotte Beauchamp, my second cousin once removed, which would make you two...well, not related in the least, I guess. Hmm. That's too bad."

"Not really." Tex looked idly at Charlotte.

"*You're* Tex Brubaker?" Charlotte sighed and let her shoulders fall.

Big Daddy Brubaker is back!
And this time his heart is set on getting
his three bachelor nephews hitched—any
way he can! Who will the lucky ladies be?
Find out in...

THE BRUBAKER BRIDES

by
Carolyn Zane

**THE MILLIONAIRE'S
WAITRESS WIFE**
(SR #1482, November 2000)

**MONTANA'S FEISTY
COWGIRL**
(SR #1488, December 2000)

**TEX'S EXASPERATING
HEIRESS**
(SR #1494, January 2001)

Watch for these uproariously funny
and wonderfully romantic tales...
only from Silhouette Romance!

COMING NEXT MONTH

#1492 BE MY BRIDE?—Karen Rose Smith
Lauren MacMillan had never forgotten sexy Cody Granger. Then
he returned to town, proposing a marriage of convenience to keep
custody of his little girl. Dare Lauren trust Cody with the heart he
had broken once before?

#1493 THE MESMERIZING MR. CARLYLE—Arlene James
An Older Man
He'd swept into her life, a handsome, charming, *wealthy* seafarer.
But struggling single gal Amber Presley had no time for romance,
though the mesmerizing Mr. Reece Carlyle seemed determined to
make her his woman. Then she learned his secret motives....

#1494 TEX'S EXASPERATING HEIRESS—Carolyn Zane
The Brubaker Brides
She'd inherited a pig! And Charlotte Beauchamp hadn't a clue how
to tame her beastly charge. Luckily, behaviorist Tex Brubaker
sprang to her rescue. But his ultimate price wasn't something
Charlotte was sure she could pay....

#1495 SECRET INGREDIENT: LOVE—Teresa Southwick
Businessman Alex Marchetti needed a chef, but was reluctant to
hire beautiful and talented Fran Carlino. They'd both been hurt
before in love, but their chemistry was undeniable. Could a
confirmed bachelor and a marriage-shy lady find love and
happiness together?

#1496 JUST ONE KISS—Carla Cassidy
Private investigator Jack Coffey claimed he was not looking for a
family, but when he collided with little Nathaniel, he found one!
As single mother Marissa Criswell nursed the dashing and surly
man back onto his feet, she looked beyond his brooding exterior
and tempted him to give her just one kiss....

#1497 THE RUNAWAY PRINCESS—Patricia Forsythe
Princess Alexis of Inbourg thought she'd found the perfect escape
from her matchmaking father. But once she arrived in Sleepy
River, she realized rancher—and boss!—Jace McTaggart was from
a very different world. Would the princess leave her castle for a
new realm—one in Jace's arms...?

CMN1200